Dead Jazz Guys *and other stories*

Dead Jazz Guys

and other stories

PHIL KAWANA

HUIA PUBLISHERS

First published in 1996 by Huia Publishers,
27 Pipitea Street, P O Box 17-335,
Wellington, Aotearoa New Zealand.

ISBN 0-908975-28-7

Designed, typeset and printed in Aotearoa New Zealand.

Contents

Dead Jazz Guys

LEE AND MIKE FIRST met in the public library. Mike was sitting cross-legged on the floor leafing through a biography of Miles Davis when he was hit on the back of the neck by a large volume on George Bernard Shaw that had somehow worked its way free of Lee's arms.

'Oh, I'm terribly sorry. Are you alright?' Lee said, squatting down to retrieve the errant tome.

'Yeah, yeah, I'm okay,' Mike muttered as he handed the book back to her. He looked up. Lee was wearing pale blue jeans, a white shirt buttoned to the collar, and a dark embroidered waistcoat. Straw-blonde hair tumbled down to just below either shoulder, framing a face that would have been strikingly pretty, were it not for a faint scar running down the right side of her jaw and disappearing beneath the shirt. She was slim, and looked to be in her early twenties. Lee smiled apologetically, and it was only then that Mike noticed that she wore no make-up. 'You could try some lighter reading, though.'

Lee's smile broadened a little, and for a brief moment her eyes dropped. 'Miles Davis?' she asked, nodding to the book he had dropped in his lap.

'Mmm. I've just started listening to his stuff. I got given a CD of his not long ago.'

'Which one? I quite like his music.'

'*Doo Bop*.'

'Right. That was his last one. He died before it came out.'

Mike nodded. He already knew this by reading the liner notes, but was quite happy to keep talking. There was a pause of a few seconds, and Lee looked as if she was about to move on.

'Are you into Shaw?' he asked.

'No, not really. I'm just picking some books up for my father.'

'Oh.'

'Um, anyway, sorry about that.'

'That's okay.'

Lee stood, smiled again, then carried on down the aisle. Mike watched her go. She held herself tall and erect, and just before she disappeared she flicked a lock of hair back over her shoulder and half turned her head to glance at him. For a brief moment their eyes met. Mike smiled, and Lee nodded slightly, then was gone.

When he got back to his flat, Mike slipped *Doo Bop* on the stereo, turned the volume up, and went into the bathroom. He looked at himself in the mirror for several minutes. By the colour of his skin and the structure of his face, he looked more like a Native American than a Maori. High cheekbones and dark eyes - legacy of his part-Samoan mother - over a straight nose, all painted a smooth and flawless coffee brown. He had a frame custom-made for an athletic build, but had inherited his parents' tendency to fat, which meant he had to work hard to keep himself looking good.

'And I do look good,' he tried to assure himself. He wasn't feeling quite that confident. In his mind was a picture of Lee, cool and collected and dressed with casual money. Not wealth, but definitely middle class. He tugged a little irritably at his tatty flannel shirt. He hoped the slacker look was going to stay in for a while longer. He wondered what she had thought of his hair. His hair was very short on top, shaved to the scalp at the back and sides, leaving a topknot that was ordered into twelve thin dreadlocks, reaching down to below his shoulder blades. 'Oh well,' he sighed, and went to find something to eat.

The following day, dole day, Mike decided to treat himself to a couple of cream buns for lunch. He was standing at the counter of the bakery waiting to be served when he heard a voice addressing him.

'I hope I didn't leave any bruises yesterday.'

Lee was standing next to him. She had a friend with her, a girl about the same age, shorter and with dark hair and bright green eyes. The friend wore too much make-up, and by the forced neatness of the dress she wore, Mike guessed that she probably worked either in a pharmacy or a bookstore. She looked at Mike, and then at Lee with the faintest dropping of her jaw.

'Hi,' said Mike as casually as he could. 'I think I survived okay.'

Lee was about to say something else when the woman behind the counter loudly asked who was next. Mike turned and paid for his cream buns and a small bottle of orange juice. He could hear Lee's friend whispering, but couldn't quite make out what it was she was saying. As he turned around again, Lee was giving her friend a swift elbow in the ribs. She looked up and caught his eye. 'We were going to have lunch in the park,' she said.

Mike had planned on going straight home, but a flirt like this was too good to pass up. 'Yeah, so was I,' he lied.

'Mind if we join you?' Lee asked as she nudged her friend towards the counter to pay for their food.

'Sure, no problem.'

'That's if, ah…'

'Nah, no problem.'

'Oh, good.' There was a pause as they both glanced over to the friend. 'Janice and I eat there every Thursday.'

'Yeah?'

'In summer. When it's not raining.'

Janice returned just in time to prevent a second awkward silence. As they left the bakery, Mike held the door open for the other two. Lee walked straight through and waited on the pavement outside. Janice glanced up at Mike with an amused smirk.

It was a five minute walk to the park. For the first minute the three of them walked quietly, Lee in the middle. Mike could feel Janice looking at him two or three times.

'My name's Lee, by the way,' said Lee. 'And this is Janice.'

'Mike. Mike Arapeta.'

'Hi, Mike.'

'Hello, Mike,' Janice said. Her voice had a slight nasal tone to it that immediately irritated Mike. He hoped she wouldn't turn out to be too talkative.

'Hi,' Mike answered. He began to feel self-conscious. He had on the same clothes he had been wearing in the library the day before, while Lee was in an expensive-looking navy jacket over a white polo neck, tan trousers and an expensive leather belt. Mike glanced around the street, hoping they wouldn't run into anyone he knew.

'So, what do you do, Mike?' Janice asked.

Mike was about to mumble 'not very much' when Lee spoke. 'He collects books on George Bernard Shaw.' Janice uttered a little grunt of surprise and looked at Mike with renewed interest. 'Janice works at Shandy's Hair. Spends all her working life finding out what everyone else is doing.' Lee and Mike both laughed. 'I was telling her last night that I had met someone with fabulous hair that she really should have seen.'

'Where did you get it done?' Janice interrupted.

'Most of it I did myself,' Mike replied. 'A friend helped me put the dreads in.'

'Really?' Janice sounded a little put out. 'It looks good.'

'Thanks.'

They reached the small park and sat down on some concrete edging that surrounded a bed of brilliantly coloured petunias.

'I did Lee's hair,' Janice said between bites of custard square.

'You did a nice job. It looks nice.'

'Thank you,' Lee and Janice both said at the same time. Lee

watched as Mike took his first bite of the cream bun and washed it down with a gulp of orange juice. 'You don't really look like a cream bun eater.'

'I'm not, normally,' Mike said, carefully wiping some cream from the corner of his mouth with the back of one hand. He was looking at her shoes as he spoke, still feeling a bit too shy to look at her directly. Brown Doc Martens. 'Just now and then. You know, monthly sugar fix.'

'Yeah. For me it's chocolates. So what do you normally eat? No, wait. Let me guess.' Mike shot a quick look at her as she paused. There was a hint of pink tongue pressing against her teeth. 'Chicken?'

'No. Fish and rice, mostly. Some chicken.'

'Oh God, you're not a tofu muncher are you?' Janice asked with a giggle.

'Yeah, sometimes.' Her tone annoyed him, and he looked squarely at her until she backed off, trying to lose herself behind the remains of her custard square. 'I like to eat healthily.' He looked down at the bun in his hand, half finished and oozing cream and sugar. 'Most of the time.'

'It's fun to be naughty every now and then,' Lee said. Somehow she had moved along the edging a little, and her knee briefly pressed against Mike's. He looked up at her again, and this time she caught his eye and held it. He could feel adrenalin starting to move through him, and he leaned forward on his knees so that they wouldn't notice if he started to get hard. Lee kept gazing at him.

'Are you a Rastafarian?' Janice asked.

'Rastas are vegetarian,' Mike said without looking at her. His attention was still fixed on Lee. 'Proper Rastas, anyway.'

'It's just that I wondered, you know, your dreadlocks...'

'I like dreads,' Mike stated, 'that's all.'

'You almost look Indian,' Lee said, 'like that guy in *Last of the Mohicans*.'

'Daniel Day Lewis' brother?' Janice asked, a degree of puzzlement in her voice.

'No,' Lee said with a sexy smirk. 'Magua, the evil one. Are you evil, Mike?'

'No. Just a little naughty from time to time.'

'Like I said, it's fun to be naughty every now and then.'

Janice stood and waited for several seconds for Lee to do likewise. When it became obvious that Lee was going to stay where she was, Janice said, 'We were going to go to Underground, to check out that jacket...'

'I haven't finished my lunch yet,' said Lee, impassively.

'I've got to be back at work in fifteen minutes!'

'You go. I'll catch up with you later.'

'Lee!' The exasperation in Janice's voice made it even more nasal. 'Lee! C'mon!'

Lee sighed. 'Oh, alright then.' She stood slowly. Janice started to walk away, but Lee paused, looking down at Mike, who was now feeling safe enough to sit upright and look back at her. 'What are you doing tonight, Mike?'

'Dunno. Taking you out somewhere?'

'Sounds good to me. Where shall I meet you?'

'Lee!' called Janice impatiently.

'How about here at seven? We can work out what to do from there.'

'You're on.' She ambled off slowly to join Janice. As she went she called back over her shoulder, 'I'll try and lose the hairdresser!'

Mike nodded. He watched as they slowly lost themselves amongst the early afternoon shoppers, Janice obviously grumpy. 'Yee ha,' Mike said softly to himself, then swallowed the last of the orange juice and tossed his rubbish into a nearby bin.

He was back at the park at ten minutes to seven that evening, clad in baggy black trousers and matching shirt. He had tied his dreads together at the nape of his neck with a bright red band. He wandered back and forwards past the petunia bed, glancing at his reflection in the showroom window across the street. 'Naughty' is what she had said, and it was how he had dressed. He had never been out with a *real* pakeha before. He had gone out with a couple of girls, Joy and Helena, but they had been raised in the same state house area as he had, and were nothing like Lee. He didn't really know what to expect, but it seemed she liked a bit of an edge. So he had dressed like a hood.

A hood with cash. Mike wished he had thought to borrow his cousin's car. He felt in his pocket. He had one hundred and fifty dollars on him. It was all the money he had. In one hand he was carrying a small box of Belgian chocolates.

Lee drove up in a white BMW at five minutes past seven. The passenger window whispered open, allowing the muted sound of a trumpet to escape from the interior of the car. Lee leaned across the front seat. 'I hope I haven't kept you waiting.'

'No, I only just got here.'

'Great. Hop in.' She opened the door for him and he got in. She turned the music down and they pulled out into the traffic. 'Miles Davis,' she said, waving a finger briefly at the stereo. 'One of his earlier recordings.'

'Nice. I, ah, bought you some chocolate.'

'Thank you.'

'They're Belgian.'

'Yum. Just put it on the back seat, will you?'

Mike looked at Lee. Again, she didn't seem to be wearing any make-up, but the scar on her jaw was so faint now, he wouldn't have spotted it if he hadn't already known it was there. She was wearing the navy jacket again, but Mike could not tell what she had on beneath it. A quick glance down revealed a white mini. Her legs were tanned and muscular. He looked up to see that she was watching him.

'Like?'

'Yes,' he said, a little embarrassed. 'You look good.'

'Thank you, Michael.'

'Actually, it's Michele. My grandfather's name. He was an Italian.'

'Italian?'

'Yeah, came over here to escape Mussolini.'

'You don't look very Italian.'

'I'm only a quarter. Half Maori, quarter Italian, quarter Samoan. What a mixture, huh?' The two of them laughed. Lee swept some hair away from her face.

'You have got Italian style, though. You look great.' Her gaze lingered on him just a little longer than it needed to. Mike smiled nervously. Lee continued, chatting away breezily as if they had known each other for years. 'My family's Dutch, mostly. There's a bit of Danish and a bit of Irish in there somewhere too.'

'What's your last name?'

Lee laughed. 'Didn't I tell you? Promise not to laugh?'

'Why? What is it?'

'Roelofs. Lee Roelofs. It was a real pain in the ass at school.'

'I bet.'

Lee put on a deep voice. 'Hey Lee, wanna *roll-off* this? Wayhey!' They stopped at traffic lights, and Lee leaned forward to turn the music up a little. 'The car belongs to my father. He's not allowed to drive any more, so I get it whenever I want.'

'Cool. It's a nice car.'

'Mmm.' The lights changed to green, and Lee slipped the BMW into drive. 'Dad had a stroke, did I say?' Her voice was a little sad, but she shrugged her shoulders and smiled across at Mike. 'So, where should we go? Have you eaten? I'm hungry.'

'No, not yet.' His fingers flicked along the edge of the money in his pocket, hoping she wouldn't suggest somewhere expensive.

'Well, how about Thai?' Lee said. 'There's a great Thai

takeaways just down here a little further, they do a fabulous chilli beef.'

Mike wondered if he was being patronised. Had she guessed he was almost broke? Lee noticed his expression, smiled and put a hand on his knee. 'I'm a chilli freak, and they have the best in town. What do you think?'

'Sounds alright to me,' Mike said. He was very conscious of her hand.

'Great, let's go.' She lifted her hand off. 'Dad was born and raised in Indonesia, and we were brought up on Asian food. I don't think I had steak, egg and chips until I was at high school.'

'That was just about all my father lived on.'

'Him and about ninety-five percent of the male population of the country.' Lee pulled the car over as she spoke, and parked outside the Thai place. It was dingy and unappealing, but the food was as good as she had said. They ate leaning against the car.

'What kind of music do you like, apart from Miles Davis?' Mike asked as they got back into the car.

'Oh, all sorts. Anything but polkas and new age drivel. What about you?'

Mike shrugged. 'Jazz, reggae - surprise, surprise - techno stuff.'

'Have you ever listened to Kraftwerk?'

'I've heard *of* them. Never listened *to* them, though.'

'You want to?' She looked at Mike, her eyebrows raised slightly. 'I've got a few of their CDs at home, and it's still a bit early to go anywhere.'

'Would your folks…'

'I don't live at home,' she said with a shake of her head. 'They bought me a place on the Parade. Great view, right next to the beach. Privileges of an only child.'

'Yeah, okay then.'

Lee's place was a fourth floor apartment that had an unobstructed view out across the harbour. Mike stood and looked out of the glass sliding door that opened on to a small balcony. Lee was hunting through a six foot high compact disc rack, looking for her copy of *Trans Europe Express*. She let out an exclamation of triumph when she located it.

'Here we go,' she said as she put it on. 'Go out on to the terrace if you want, I'll get us a drink. What'll you have? Vodka, rum or wine's all I've got at the moment. There might be some orange juice in the fridge.'

'Vodka and orange, if you've got it. Just straight vodka's okay though.'

'Coming up.' Lee disappeared into the kitchen. She joined Mike out on the terrace a few minutes later. She handed him a tumbler of vodka and orange. The sky over the harbour was a pale blue, just beginning to develop the darker hues of twilight. 'Here you go. Great view, huh? I really like it out here. It's brilliant when it's dark.'

'I bet. Thanks.' He took a sip. She had mixed it strong. 'What do you do for a living?'

'A bit of this, a bit of that, a lot of sponging off Dad.' She leaned against the railings and regarded him. There was a gentle breeze that blew her hair behind her. 'You must think I'm a spoilt little rich girl.'

'It's good work if you can get it,' he smiled and lifted his glass again. 'Cheers.'

Lee lifted her glass of wine in reply, and sipped from it slowly. 'I'm glad I ran into you today.'

'Are you?' Mike wondered if now was the time.

'Yes,' Lee said, and held eye contact for several seconds. She tossed back the rest of her wine and started inside, beckoning Mike to follow her. 'When I described you to Janice, she thought you're probably a drug dealer. Are you, Mike?'

'No.' He felt like he was being made fun of, and wondered

what was going on inside her head. She looked a little disappointed. 'Would you like me to be?'

Lee just smiled. 'I've got some hash and some ecstasy stashed away if you'd like?'

'Ecstasy's a bit too yuppie for me.'

Lee laughed and poured them both another drink. 'Maybe later then. I used the last of the orange juice before, I'm afraid. Is it okay straight?'

'Fine.'

'Good,' she said as she handed him a second glass of vodka. 'So what do *you* do to make your way?'

'Officially, I'm a government statistic. Unofficially, I do bone-carving.'

'Really? Do you sell them locally?'

'I've got a cousin in Taupo, he sells them to tourists up there. I send them up there, and he brings me down some cash once a month. Under the table.'

They sat on a settee that faced out over the harbour. Kraftwerk pulsed from speakers in each corner of the room. Lee turned sideways and leaned back against the arm of the settee. She looked at Mike over the rim of her wine glass. Her jacket slipped open, and Mike realised the white mini was a high-necked one-piece dress. Lee eased her legs up onto the seat so that they pressed against his thigh. Slowly, cautiously, Mike reached down and began to gently stroke her shins.

'That feels nice,' she said and straightened out her legs over his. She kicked her shoes off over the end of the settee. 'Keep going.'

Mike put his drink down on an end table, and then ran his hands slowly up and down her calves. Lee nestled down in the seat, purring happily and closing her eyes. Mike had to almost turn around to reach her feet, which he massaged gently. When he turned back towards her, Lee's eyes were open again. He slid his hands up past her knees, over the outer sides of her thighs until the tips of his fingers stopped just inside the hem of her dress. Lee reached back over her head, placing her drink on the table behind her. Her lips parted, and she reached out to touch Mike's neck. She slipped her fingers under his shirt and on to his chest. Her hands were warm and soft. 'You have nice skin,' Lee said.

Mike eased his fingers out from her dress and slid them up her sides, underneath her jacket, leaning forward as he went. Soon he was lying, half behind her, his hands gently touching her back, his nose against her cheek. He could feel her breath against his cheek, and her hands clasping behind his neck to pull him closer to her. He slid his lips along Lee's jaw to her ear, tugged softly at her earlobe. 'I want you,' she whispered.

They kissed, slowly at first, nuzzling and nibbling at each other's lips, but as the passion built, they quickly began to explore mouth, teeth, tongue. Lee wriggled her way on top of Mike, took his hands in hers and pulled him up off the settee. She held him close and whispered softly. 'I had an accident when I was a kid. There are still scars...'

Mike understood her choice of clothes then. He held her lightly by the waist and kissed her. 'It's okay.'

Afterwards, as they lay tired and content in the shadows, Mike found himself thinking about jazz. Exploration, experimentation, exultation. It seemed the perfect accompaniment for the moment. He padded through to the stereo, hunted through the rack until he found a disc by John Coltrane and Don Cherry. He slipped it into the player and stood in the semi-darkness, listening. Dead jazz guys, electronically resurrected to perform their musical miracles just for him and Lee. He wondered how long a dead man could play. Notes slithered through the room and out across the water like a mirrored cobra, flexing and twisting, reflecting back the lights of the city. Mike pondered whether it was all doomed to just fade away with the dawn of the living. He went back into the bedroom. Lee was lying across the bed like a reclining ivory sculpture.

'You're beautiful,' he said.

Lee sat up, hugged her legs to her chest and rested her chin on her knees. Her eyes followed him as he sat next to her. 'Can I ask a personal question?' she asked.

'Sure.'

'You ever slept with a Pakeha before?'

'No. Believe it or not.'

'I believe it.'

'Do you think that's strange?'

'I don't know. No, probably not. I've never slept with someone I hadn't been seeing for months before, so I guess…'

'Yeah, I suppose.'

Lee let go of her legs, shuffled over and kissed Mike again. She rested one hand on the back of his head, fingers twisting through his dreadlocks. 'Do you want to stay the night?'

'Yeah.'

'Good. I'd like that.'

In the darkness, they touched something together, the edges of a fantasy. At some time they would have to awake, return to the deadness of the everyday, enshrouded by elevator music. But for now, angels arose from the grave to serenade them. From the lounge, John Coltrane's saxophone and Don Cherry's trumpet writhed and danced around each other. Supple, sinewy and alive.

Moko Carved in Rimu

ANDREW'S GRANDFATHER SAT on his chair on the verandah, sleeping. Every now and then he would mumble something, or his mouth would twitch like a kahawai caught on a line, and then he would settle back down and resume his dreaming. It seemed to Andrew that was all you did at his age, sleep and dream.

Andrew was sitting in the doorway, listening to NWA on his discman as he leaned back against the jamb, facing the old man. His grandfather was short, and his face so heavily lined by a long and hard life that the wrinkles looked like a moko carved in rimu. His hair was still dark, but he had long ago gone bald on top and ever since had combed what locks remained across the shiny pate. It looked ludicrous, always had done, but no one had been rude enough to tell him to his face. Everyone called him Karu.

I wonder what I'll look like when I'm that old? Andrew was thinking. Certainly, the two looked nothing alike. Where his grandfather was short, Andrew was over six feet tall. While Karu tried in vain to disguise his baldness, the other shaved his head to the scalp, emulating some American sporting hero. They were as different to look at as family can get, yet were closer to each other than anyone else in the whanau.

Earlier in the morning, Karu had walked into the lounge while Andrew and his friend Isaac were watching a video, an action movie called *Surviving the Game*. He had sat down and watched it with them for a while, then asked who the actor with the dreadlocks was.

'Ice-T,' Isaac answered.

Karu laughed. 'Iced Tea? What sort of a dumb name is that?'

'*Ice*-T, Karu,' Andrew explained. 'T like the letter, not the drink. Ice-T. He made it as a rapper first, then started doing movies. He's cool.'

'Ne?' was all Karu said.

'Speak English, Karu,' Andrew said. 'Dad never sent us to kohanga.'

'More's the pity, more's the pity,' Karu muttered as he got up and walked away.

After the video, Andrew and Isaac had played one-on-one out by the carport, where Andrew's father had put up a basketball hoop two years before. Isaac left just before lunch. He had to go home and mow the lawns for his mother.

Karu woke up and, as he often did these days, had to look around for a few seconds before he remembered where he was. Soon, he felt Andrew watching him. He swivelled around in his chair. Karu turned off the compact disc.

'Yes? What do you want?'

'What was it like when you were young, Karu?'

Karu smiled. 'You mean back when your grandmother and I were hunting moas?'

'No, really, Karu. What was it like?'

'What was it like? It was different, very different. When I was little, we lived on the farm next to the marae - you know, that old house next to your Aunty Livy's place? We only used to speak pakeha at school and in town. I got caned more than once for talking te reo at school. Nowadays, you can't even train to be a bloody nurse unless you can whaikorero. And we're still stuck with a Maori Affairs minister who doesn't know his cake from his armpit!'

Karu picked up his tobacco pouch and started to roll himself a cigarette. Once he had lit it and taken his first drag, he looked over to his grandson. 'It hasn't been the same since the war. We all came back changed.'

'Is that what you dream about, Karu?'

'Sometimes. I was a bit older than you when I went away. You may not think you're a kid, and I didn't think I was then either. But some of the things I saw when we got to Italy... When I got back, nothing seemed the same. We moved into the city to get better jobs, and better schools for your father. They taught him to speak properly and make money. I tell you what, though,' he said, leaning forward with a grin, lowering his voice so as not to be overheard, 'he still can't tell puha from fat hen!' He laughed for several seconds, then settled back in his seat, looking out over the carefully tended gardens. 'My boy is nearly fifty years old, and he can't pick puha without my help,' he said, sadly and softly to himself.

Andrew fiddled uncomfortably. Karu sighed, and turned back to his grandson. 'And you young fellas today, you all run around like you were living in Harlem or something. I hate to shatter your illusions, Andrew, but you're a Maori, not a Negro.'

'They don't say Negro any more, Karu. They say African-American.'

'Is that so? African-American? Well, whatever. You don't seem to know who you are any more. Your father's the same. And as for me, well I'm just some old fart who always dreams about the good old days.' He paused, then looked seriously at Andrew. 'The good old days were bullshit. Always have been. It's just that people are scared of growing old. You, you think you'll always be young, but it'll be gone before you know it. And you'll look around for something else to fill the gap that your youth has left. We all do it. Your father, he's finally getting around to learning to speak his own language, "rediscovering his roots" he calls it.' He pointed a finger at Andrew to emphasise his point.

'That's the problem with life now. No sense of place or of belonging until it's too late. I grew up knowing who I was and where I came from. Took it for granted, I suppose. Brought your father up in the pakeha world cos I thought that's what he needed. And now…?' Karu shook his head slowly. 'And now, this Polynesian-New Zealander is going to the pub.'

Karu pulled himself up out of the chair with a grunt and went inside. Andrew turned the CD back on, stretched out a little and closed his eyes, making sure he left enough room for Karu to get past when he left for the hotel.

Five minutes later something hard tapped him on the leg. Andrew opened one eye and saw Karu leaning over him. Andrew pulled his headphones off.

'Something for you,' Karu said. 'You're old enough to take it now, I think.' He held out his walking stick for Andrew.

'What's that for? I can walk.'

'This is what it's for,' Karu said, and fished a pocket knife out of his trousers. He fumbled about until he had extracted the larger of the two blades, and then cut a circular mark around the stick about halfway up. He held the stick out again until Andrew took it. 'See that cut. That's history. That's a place. That's me. Keep it, give it to your own mokopuna when they're old enough to begin to understand.'

'I don't get it,' Andrew said, puzzled. He ran his finger along the carved mark, then noticed that there were several other marks in the cane, half hidden by the age of the polish. Nine or ten circles, like miniature carvings.

'You will, son, you will,' Karu said, and walked down the footpath, whistling happily.

The Rise and Fall of Skankadelica

SKANKADELICA HELD THEIR FIRST practice in the double garage where Hemi Kira, the lead guitarist, slept. His brother, Dennis, and his girlfriend owned the house, but they had sold their car months ago, which left plenty of room for the band's gear. Apart from Hemi, there were four other Kiras in Skankadelica - Hemi's brothers Rua and Charlie on bass and rhythm, and cousins Chantelle and Jimmy on vocals and percussion. As well as these five, there was also Rogue Karaitiana on drums and 'Prof' Mason on keyboards.

The first practice was held on the first Sunday after rugby league finished for the year. There had been talk about forming a band for months, but it had been put off and put off while Rua, Rogue and Charlie tried to crack a place in the provincial rep side. Rogue got named for two games as a reserve forward, and even got a run in the second game, against Canterbury B. He lasted fifteen minutes and then broke his arm while completing an illegal high tackle. It put him out for the rest of the season.

Prof and Rogue arrived just beforé midday to start setting up the gear. Rogue had a five-piece Tama kit, with Zildjian cymbals he'd flogged from a cousin in Hamilton. Prof's rig consisted of an old Roland Juno 106 analog synth of his own, plus a Hohner Clavinet and a Rockit amplifier that actually belonged to his girlfriend Sonia's father. He didn't have a stand for the keyboards yet, and so he had to talk Dennis Kira into letting him have the kitchen table for the afternoon. Once the keys and the drums were set up, Rogue and Prof started running extension cords all over the floor and plugging in the guitar amps. Just after they arrived, Hemi had left to grab some spare guitar strings from Ricky Collins, yet another of the Kira cousins who had his own band. By the time he got back, the others had all arrived and were already onto their third joint for the day. As well as the band members, there was Chantelle's latest boyfriend and her friend Aroha, two other girls from around the corner, Rogue's mate Chris, and Rogue's uncle John, who had a rock 'n' roll band and who reckoned he could get Skankadelica a few gigs if they were good enough.

Hemi was supposed to be in charge of the practice, but there was still a half hour argument over what songs they were going to do. Eventually they decided on a list of seven songs: *Them Belly Full, Stir It Up, Trenchtown Rock* and *Time Will Tell* by Bob Marley, *Johnny B. Goode* à la Peter Tosh, *I and I* by Bob Dylan and a skankified version of *Rock In Peace* by AC/DC. There were the inevitable chants from Prof and Rogue to do one of their own instrumentals, and for a few minutes Chantelle threatened to walk out if they didn't do something by either Sonny Lovett or Judy Mowatt. She was eventually pacified by Rua, who slipped her a bullet and promised they'd do one at the next practice.

When Skankadelica finally started playing *Trenchtown Rock* it was almost 2:45. They had originally planned to begin at one o'clock. It took Charlie, Rua and Rogue three attempts before they got a groove going, and then Prof and Hemi started adding layers over the top. Finally, Jimmy stepped up to the microphone and unleashed his velvet-smooth voice.

'One good thing about music,
When it 'its, you feel no shame…'

Charlie and Hemi both stopped playing. Rua and Rogue smiled to each other, but kept going.

'"Pain", not "shame",' Hemi yelled over the top of the rhythm section. 'It should be "When it hits, you feel no pain."'

'Oh, yeah, right,' mumbled Jimmy. He scribbled a note in the old schoolbook he kept his words in, and Skankadelica started again.

The second song they attempted was *Johnny B. Goode*. Prof and Hemi were already disagreeing about how loud the keyboards should be, and who should be playing which line. Uncle John stepped in and offered to act as mixer, while Hemi laid down the rules regarding what Prof should and should not play. For the first half of *Johnny B. Goode*, Prof sulked and turned his synth off.

By four o'clock, they had only gotten through four songs, but they had to stop because Dennis' girlfriend wanted the kitchen table back. Jimmy, Chantelle and her boyfriend went home to grab some tea, while Hemi and John went around to John's house to talk about gigs. Rua and Rogue carried on playing, trying out different grooves. Charlie and Aroha disappeared. Prof tried to teach the two girls from around the corner how to play *Für Elise*. Rua, Rogue and Chris finally packed up and left a little after six o'clock. An hour later, Hemi came back to find Prof and one of the girls from around the corner hard at it in his bed.

The next Friday, all the band plus Uncle John - who by now had become 'Uncle' to everyone - met at the Railway Hotel. Prof was the last to arrive, and when he finally did turn up he was sporting a black eye, much to everyone's amusement.

'What happened to you?' chuckled Rua. 'Chantelle open the door while you were having a nohi through the keyhole?'

'Nah, I bet Sonia just closed her legs too quickly!' suggested Rogue.

'I reckon I know,' said Chantelle. 'Sonia found out about that girl you went with last Sunday.'

'Yeah,' Prof said sheepishly. 'I got the full 'I never want to see you again as long as I live' speech. So much for the clavinet and the amp.'

The others laughed, and Rogue passed Prof a beer.

'So, what was her name?' Rogue asked. Prof just mumbled.

'What was that?' Rogue asked again.

'I don't know. I can't remember.'

'What an asshole,' Chantelle said with obvious disgust. 'Her name is Terri. Her and I were in the same class at school. She's nicer than you deserve. You better watch yourself there, boy. Her brother's a cop in Wanganui.'

'Oh shit.'

'The band now has its first groupie!'

For the next hour they argued over a name. The first suggestion was 'The K Band' because of the Kiras and Karaitiana, but Prof objected because his initial wasn't in there, and both Jimmy and Rua thought it sounded dumb anyway. Prof suggested 'The Ganja Foundation' but Uncle John said it would just get them harassed by the cops. Eventually it was Chantelle who suggested Skankadelica. They took a vote, and it was adopted five votes to two, with Uncle John abstaining. Hemi was officially appointed as being in charge of the music, Rogue and Prof in charge of the gear, Chantelle responsible for making sure everyone was at the right place at the right time. Uncle John became the official gig-finder. Jimmy and Rua were appointed as drivers, and Charlie was given the most important job: ensuring a constant supply of marijuana. Skankadelica Inc was born.

The second practice was much better organised than the first. Reduced to just the one keyboard, Prof could balance his synthesiser on the top of the amplifier he had borrowed from Ricky Collins. This meant that there was no need for Dennis' table, allowing them to practice right through until seven o'clock, when they had to stop so that Dennis' daughter could go to sleep.

Aroha was there, spending most of the day sitting on Hemi's bed watching Charlie's every move. Terri arrived about two o'clock and made a beeline straight for Prof. Rua and Rogue let out mocking whoops which Prof and Terri both pretended not to hear. Between songs, Hemi wandered over and told them to leave his bed alone this time. All in all, it was decided afterwards, it was a very good day.

The following Wednesday, a meeting at the Railway was called. Once everyone had arrived, Uncle John told them he had scored Skankadelica a support gig with Ricky Collins' band Axatak at a big party at a woolshed up Andersons Valley that coming Saturday. There was no money, but they would get a keg of beer and a bottle of Bacardi for Chantelle.

Skankadelica's first gig started off a bit shakily when Jimmy got the words to *Trenchtown Rock* wrong again and Rua broke his D string near the end of their second song and had to borrow Axatak's bass. They started playing at ten o'clock, and did a twenty minute set. Axatak came on next for an hour, and then Skankadelica did a second set. Because they only had thirty minutes of music, they resorted to an extra long dub based around *Knockin' on Heaven's Door.* Prof was the only one who knew the words to the verses, but he couldn't remember which order they were supposed to go in, so he would wander up to the microphone and sing one verse, then everyone would join in and sing '*knock, knock, knocking on heaven's door*' over and over again until they got sick of it, after which Hemi would start on a guitar solo.

Apart from a little incident during Axatak's last set involving Charlie and some guy's girlfriend in the back of Rua's Ford Falcon, everything else went off quite satisfactorily. Chantelle polished off three-quarters of her bottle of Bacardi, threw up on her boyfriend and then passed out on the way home. It was decided to save the keg for the following afternoon so that no one would miss out or get picked up by the cops for drunk driving. Rather than leave it in the cars, everyone - except for Chantelle who was still out cold - helped unload the gear into Hemi's garage when they got back into town just before five o'clock. Practice was cancelled in favour of a four o'clock barbecue and keg-emptying.

Half an hour after she arrived at the barbecue - minus her boyfriend - Chantelle started hassling the others about being a reggae band in which she was the only one with dreadlocks. Rua, who had been at Dennis' for some time and was already drunk, laughed at her and then disappeared inside. When he returned, Rua sported a clean-shaven head. Charlie and Hemi were so taken with the idea that they both went and shaved their heads too. Chantelle snorted in disgust and went off to a corner with Dennis' girlfriend and the two of them polished off the remains of the Bacardi.

At the band meeting at the Railway on the Friday, both Jimmy and Rogue had dreads. Chantelle looked at Prof and raised her eyebrows questioningly.

'So, what are you gonna do, boy?'

'Wait and see,' Prof smiled, 'wait and see.'

On the basis of their relative success in Andersons Valley, Uncle John had scored a second gig, a fundraiser for a local kohanga reo in early December. Due to various reasons, Skankadelica only managed two more practices before the gig. The night before, Prof phoned Chantelle to let her know that he'd be a little late and wouldn't be able to set up the gear, but he would be there in time for their seven o'clock start.

When he and Terri walked into the hall at quarter to seven, a brief silence fell over the crowd. Terri was dressed in an incredibly short mini skirt and a very brief halter top. But it was Prof himself that stopped everyone in their tracks. Rising up from the top of his head like some kind of kaleidoscopic fountain were seven braids of hair, one dyed red, one blue, one green, one blonde, one a shocking pink and the other two left Prof's natural dark brown. He wore mirror-lensed shades, a sleeveless, zebra-patterned t-shirt with several tears revealing the smooth brown skin beneath, red leather trousers so tight that Chantelle later said she could count the hairs on his legs, fastened with two silk scarves, one white and one purple, twisted together and trailing down one thigh. His feet were bare.

'Bloody hell!' whispered Hemi.

Prof swaggered over to the rest of the band, enjoying the feel of everyone watching him.

'I was expecting the Prof,' Charlie said, 'not "the artist formerly known as Prince!"'

Prof wiggled his head at Chantelle, his braids writhing like an acid-tripping Medusa.

Later that night, after Skankadelica had played, a couple of guys from out of town were going to take Prof outside and beat him up because they thought he was gay, but when they were told he was going with Terri of the ultra mini and long legs, they decided he was okay and took him outside and spotted some hash with him instead.

Charlie and Aroha disappeared early, so when Skankadelica was asked to hop up and play another set, Ricky Collins sat in. He was there because his wife was one of the kohanga teachers. Chantelle's boyfriend arrived during the second set. It was the first time anyone had seen him since Chantelle had chundered on him in Andersons Valley. She left the stage halfway through *Lively Up Yourself* and didn't reappear until the next band meeting at the Railway. Hemi, Ricky and Uncle John left just before midnight to catch another band playing in town. Jimmy got into a fight with Dennis and stormed off not long after Hemi and the others had left. That left Rua, Rogue and Prof to load up the gear and take it back to Hemi's. Terri caught a ride with them, and her and Prof disappeared as soon as the last amp was in the garage.

It was at the meeting at the Railway the following Friday that everything started to fall apart. Chantelle announced that she was going to go to Sydney with her boyfriend. Hemi said that Dennis was still so pissed off with Jimmy that either he left the band or Skankadelica - and Hemi - had to find somewhere else to stay. Jimmy shrugged his shoulders, finished his beer, then walked away. Uncle John said that their next gig wouldn't be until mid-January, so it was decided that it was in everyone's interest to take a three-week break, and then practice again in the new year.

The first scheduled practice of the new year was postponed because Rogue and Charlie were both at a pre-season league training camp. Uncle John said that didn't matter too much anyway, because the gig had fallen through and he didn't have anything else lined up for them yet.

On January 12th, Rua announced that he was leaving Skankadelica to play for Axatak.

Two days later, Rogue called everyone together at the Railway. He was highly excited, and greeted everyone as they arrived with a hug and a bottle of beer. 'I've been picked up!' he said, struggling to get the words past a huge smile. 'I got spotted by a scout at the pre-season camp, and I've signed up with the Rochdale Hornets in England. I leave in March!'

Everyone shared his excitement. It looked like he had cracked the big time. The party didn't fizzle out until sometime around seven o'clock the following night.

Skankadelica was now down to just Hemi, Prof and Charlie. Charlie said he was happy to swap over on to bass, and that Aroha was a pretty good drummer. It was agreed to give her a go. Skankadelica Mark II practised for the first time on January 20th. Much to everyone's surprise, the results were pretty good. They sounded quite different to the original line-up, but good all the same.

On the 23rd, Terri told Prof that she was pregnant.

On the morning of the 27th, Charlie went to church with Aroha's brother and arrived at practice that afternoon to share the news that he had become a born-again Christian and was leaving the band to dedicate his life to the Lord. Aroha swore at her brother and stomped away, slamming the door noisily as she went.

Skankadelica disbanded at 1:23 pm on the 27th of January.

Redemption

WE ONLY HAD the one capsule left, and so we broke it open and carefully tipped its contents out on to a saucer. Jaffa grabbed a drinking straw from one of the drawers, and we carefully divided the tiny granules up into two even piles before snorting them. I had a bit of a cold, and so it took two or three snorts to clean up my share. Then, while we waited for it to take effect, I rolled us a five-paper joint which we smoked out on the back step, seeing as Jaffa's brother didn't like us smoking inside.

'What did ya say that stuff was?' Jaffa asked between tokes.

'Can't remember,' I said. 'Dog did tell me, but I was off my face at the time. He said he had a whole box of the stuff, and we could score a couple of bags anytime.'

'Cool.'

The joint was half gone, which meant there would be a good build up of resin in the roach, so I flipped it around and held it, burning end towards me.

'Shotgun time,' I said, closing my lips around the joint, being careful not to burn my tongue the way Jaffa had the first time she had tried it. She leaned forward until her lips were half an inch from the end of the roach, and then I exhaled, blowing a stream of smoke into her eagerly sucking mouth. We swapped roles two or three times until the roach was too small, then I pulled out my bag to see how much grass I was still holding. There was maybe enough for a real small doobie. I couldn't be bothered with something that little.

'Come down here,' Jaffa said, and lead me down towards the back gate. Beyond it were the garages and sheds for her brother's house and the place next door. They used to be power board houses, and had heaps of outbuildings for all the linemen's gear. Jaffa had turned one of the garages into a crash pad. Sometimes I would sleep out here when it wasn't safe to go home. Jaffa's unfinished tukutuku panel stood off to one side, and I had painted a giant koru design on the opposing wall. Jaffa's niece had been in too, and pinned her Jonah Lomu posters to the wall by the old mattress that we used as a bed. Jaffa pulled them down carefully, folded them and placed them on the bench. She started pulling bits and pieces out of a cupboard while I stretched out on the bed.

'Here we go,' she said, and pulled out a large plastic bag. I could smell the glue before she got within reach of me. 'This'll really fuck you,' she giggled. She took a few deep chugs then held out the bag towards me.

'Nah, bugger that,' I said. 'I'd rather get fucked by you.'

'Just be patient,' she said, before taking a few more deep chugs. Jaffa dropped the bag on the old grey blanket at the foot of the mattress and then lay down on top of me. 'What you gotta do this week?'

'The old man wants me to go down to Porirua and work for Uncle Roto. Fuck! He reckons I either get a job or he's gonna kick me out.'

'Sleep here.'

'When I'm here, who wants to sleep?' I slipped one hand down the back of Jaffa's jeans. She squirmed a little to let me get in a bit further. She kissed me, but the taste of glue in her mouth was so strong I nudged her head away and started to nip and bite her neck. After a little while she sat up, shuffled down until she was sitting across my thighs, and then slowly, teasingly, stripped off her shirt and bra. 'Time for Redemption,' she said.

Redemption was our own private game. Jaffa went first. She turned around so that I could see the five long, thin welts across her back, three of them ending in deeper cuts.

'Dad saw that picture that Huia took of us doing it,' she said softly. I reached out and touched the marks gently with the tips of my fingers.

'It's got nothing to do with the bastard,' I said. 'You don't live there any more.'

Jaffa looked at me over her shoulder. 'Makes no difference to him. He came around and brought the whip with him.'

The whip was a length of electrical cord her father had pinched from a building site years ago. He had seen some film where Jesus got whipped with a cat-o'-nine-tails and he had made his own version. He had stripped back the last foot or so of the cord to free the three insulated wires within. At the end of these wires he had taken off the plastic coating and tied the copper wire into knots. When he hit the kids with it, the copper wire would slash into the softer skin at the side of the back.

I guided Jaffa off me and on to her stomach. The red marks seemed to glow in the harsh light. I leaned over her and started to kiss her back, running my tongue along the raised ridges left by her father's whip. There were older scars there too, pale tracks across the toffee-coloured skin. I ran my fingers along them, tracing out a fan-shaped pattern that broadened on her right side. Once I had kissed all five of the fresh marks, I lifted her hair off her shoulders and kissed the back of her neck.

'My turn,' I said, and pulled off my jeans. My thighs were latticed with deep, black-brown bruises. 'Mum and Tony again.' Tony, my older brother, would hold me down while Mum laid in with the jug cord.

'What for this time?'

'I forgot to put some salt in with the poroporo.' When Mum hit the Jim Beam, it didn't take much to set her off.

Jaffa touched her lips gently to the bruises. With the faintest of suckings, she drew out the pain we felt. By kissing each other's wounds, we told each other that there were other ways of living.

'Fuck them,' I said, biting back the urge to cry. Jaffa could see the bruises, but I would never let her see me cry.

The stuff we had snorted earlier was starting to kick in. Colours started to separate, and each sound became an object that we could see moving through the air. We took off the rest of our clothes and lay down together, running our hands slowly over each other. I could feel Jaffa's breath enshrouding me.

We had it off for what seemed like hours. Afterwards, as the pill started to wear off, Jaffa looked a little green.

'You okay?' I asked.

'I'll be right,' she said. 'I'm just a little late, y'know?' She sat up, hunched over on the side of the mattress, holding her stomach. 'Maybe I should have skipped the glue.'

I didn't answer. I was wondering about sneaking home and grabbing my stash, then coming back for another screw. Jaffa went outside for a while, and I could hear her throwing up in the weeds. I decided against going home. I felt like sleeping.

Jaffa came back in, turned off the light and then lay down next to me. I grabbed the grey blanket and pulled it over us. We both fell asleep quickly.

When I woke up, the sky was just starting to lighten. Jaffa was still sound asleep on her stomach, so I went inside and made us a cup of tea. When I got back to the garage, she hadn't moved.

'Hey, wake up lazy. Tea. C'mon.' I leaned over her to shake her shoulder. It was then that I noticed all the vomit. I dropped her tea on the concrete floor, the cup shattered and sprayed its contents over my feet. I yanked off the blanket and pulled her face out of the spew. She felt cold.

I cleaned her up as much as I could, wiping her up with the blanket. I held her close to me, tried to warm her with my own body heat. She just flopped against me limply. I kissed her eyes, her cheek, her lips, her breasts, tried to buy her back with my kisses. She could not wake up. It was simply too late.

I gave up just after dawn. I dressed Jaffa carefully, lay her on the mattress with her head away from the pool of vomit, and then kissed her goodbye. Taking one of the broken pieces of cup off the floor, I gouged a deep cut across my chest, dabbed some of the blood with a finger and anointed her lips with it. Then I turned away and went to tell her brother.

The Scheme

IT WAS JUST another work scheme really. You know the kind of thing, do this or do that for no apparent or lasting reason for six months, then back on the dole while another group gets a turn doing the same thing. Maybe it's clearing gorse away from around the reservoir, always using a slasher so that the gorse grows back again after a few months and gives the next scheme something to do. Never a proper job, just something so that the government can play with figures and convince the middle class (you know, the ones that vote) that they really *are* doing something about unemployment, that the economic upturn really *is* just around the corner.

Yeah, right.

Anyway, on this particular day, on this particular scheme, we were clearing gorse. We were supposed to tidy up a little country graveyard first, then clear along either side of the nearby railway lines for five kilometres. The day got off to a slow start, and the supervisor, Darryl, learned an important lesson: don't expect a bunch of superstitious Maoris to clean up an old graveyard.

You see, the thing was that this was a really old cemetery, and most of the gravestones were broken and toppled, and it was absolutely overrun by weeds.

'Cemetery this old,' I said to Carl, Lucky and Blackass, 'there's bound to be heaps of unmarked graves.'

'Bugger that,' muttered Blackass.

'I ain't walking over no grave,' said Carl.

We looked at each other in agreement. We were all standing at the crest of a small rise. Behind us, the road weaved its way back into town. Below us, Darryl and the three other pakehas in the work gang had already started clearing away the gorse and the lupin. Darryl looked up at us and waved his slasher.

'Move your asses!' he yelled. 'I want this cleared out by ten!'

'We're not going in!' I yelled back. 'Not until we know where all the graves are!'

'Wutha matter, black boyth? Thcared of ghotht-th?' lisped Harry. He was short, obese and obnoxious, with false teeth that fitted so badly they looked like he had stolen them from a pygmy. He probably had. His face had a constant sneer, and his voice that peculiar whining tone that identified him as a Grade A Asshole. Carl answered him in our usual fashion. He threw something at him, sheep shit I think.

'Are you refusing to work?' Darryl asked. I could tell by his tone that he was still in a good mood, so I could afford to push it a little.

'On cultural grounds,' I said. 'We don't mind working when we know where the graves are. But we will not walk over the top of anyone's grave.' Actually, to be honest, it didn't really worry me that much. But it *was* Monday morning.

'Bloody Maoris,' Darryl muttered, running already dirty fingers through his light brown hair. 'Alright, we'll clean this up, but you guys have to do the first half along the rails yourself. Okay?'

I looked at the others. They just shrugged their shoulders. 'Okay,' I agreed. The four of us walked down to the bottom of the slope and sat just outside the gate. While the others worked, we played club euchre.

About a quarter to ten, we decided it was time to start along the rails. Darryl told us we had to go as far as the next road, and he and the others would meet us there in the van. We picked up our slashers and were on our way, me and Carl on one side of the tracks, Lucky and Blackass on the other. Any gorse or lupin growing between the tracks and the fences had to be cut.

Anyone who has had anything to do with gorse realises eventually that you can't clear it permanently armed just with a slasher. A slasher is little more than a cleaver-like blade mounted on an axe handle. Gorse is a disgustingly hardy plant, and always grows back. I'm not sure whether it grows from the old stumps, or from seeds, but it grows back all the same. We had all realised it long ago. Blackass, who was somewhere in his forties, had known it longer than anyone, and told us almost every day how pointless this was. But at least it was something to do, and we'd get no money otherwise.

Still, it is a real pain in the neck doing something you know serves no real purpose other than making some politician in Wellington look better. Let's just say that motivation was never terribly high.

Carl and I worked as a team, either of us taking alternate stands of gorse. About half a kilometre along there was a small patch of manuka saplings, none more than a couple of feet high. We slashed them too. Halfway through the first cutting, Lucky stopped, dropped his slasher and laid his ear to the rail. 'Ugh!' he called. 'The steel-horse tracks talk!'

'What you hear-um, Running Dog?'

'White-face Harry, scratching bum.'

Carl laughed. 'He'll lose his fingers!'

'He'll lose his arm,' Blackass corrected.

We ambled on. It was a reasonably nice day, a bit cloudy and the westerly was threatening to build up to a decent gust, but for the moment it was warm. The last few months had been hot and dry, and the coolish breeze was quite welcome. There wasn't very much growth along the tracks, and so mostly we just walked and talked. Lucky was doing a gripe about Darryl. The two had never gotten on, and now that Lucky had only a few weeks left on the scheme, he was counting the days until his escape.

We were about halfway to the road when we emerged from a second cutting and rounded a bend in the tracks. To the right, the side that Carl and I were working, was a basin-shaped depression, maybe thirty feet across, packed so tight with mature gorse that we probably could have walked across the top of it to the neighbouring paddock. Carl and I both let out a groan at the same time. When they saw it, Lucky and Blackass, overcome by sympathy, just about wet their pants laughing.

'Maybe we could just leave it,' I said hopefully.

'No way,' Carl said. 'Bill Michaels always checks up on where we've been.'

Bill Michaels was Darryl's boss, and we were already in trouble with him. We hadn't really done anything, but by sad misfortune one of the other guys, Richie, used to go out with his daughter and it had all ended badly. From the day Richie had started on the scheme, Bill had been riding us.

So, reluctantly, Carl and I started hacking our way in. It was close to impossible. The sides of the depression were steep, and we had to kick footholds in the side to stop ourselves from falling. Falling into gorse is something to be avoided wherever possible, I tell you. They say that in Britain they use it for hedges, and the thorns on it are soft and more just a nuisance than anything else. On a good stand of gorse here, though, there are thorns the size of a stallion's danglies, and twice as dangerous.

We'd slash away at a bush, then gently ease each fallen piece out of our way. Get a fresh foothold, then swing again. After my second bush, I looked across the basin. It seemed to have grown till it was about a mile across. I imagined purgatory must be something like this.

'Hey, Carl, got some matches?'

'You reckon?'

'Bloody oath! Otherwise, we'll be here all day. She's dry enough.'

'You can do it, here. Just wait till I'm out, okay?' He tossed over a box of matches. I had to go fishing through the undergrowth beneath my feet to retrieve them.

Carl scrambled up on the edge by the tracks. I held the matches in my mouth and cut away the growth until I was a little closer to the middle of the basin, able to get at the tinder-dry wood that had been sheltered at its centre. Then I struck a match and set fire to it.

What I had forgotten to take into account were four important factors. First, gorse at any time is very combustible. Second, and tied in strongly to the first, is that it had been a long, hot, dry summer. The gorse ignited like paper, and a good-sized section was soon a roaring blaze. I backed off along the path I had hacked, squinting my eyes against the heat. The third thing I had overlooked was the gusty westerly, which blew some of the fire back towards me.

But the most important thing I had overlooked was the fourth and final factor. I was in a steep-sided basin. I was reminded of this little piece of information when I turned to get away from the burn-off and was confronted with a short, fiery corridor that ended in a wall of steep, slippery earth.

I think the word is panic.

I uttered a few words that would have made my mother faint, then got myself through the corridor faster than curry through a honky. The side of the basin was a bigger ask though. I tried to use the steps I had dug with my heels on the way down, but I was in such a hurry that I slipped, and obliterated them. A slasher handle appeared before my eyes.

'Grab hold of this, you silly bugger,' Carl called from above me.

I did as I was bid, and I scrabbled my way out of there. As I lay beside the railway tracks, I could smell the soles of my boots melting. It was a vaguely disgusting smell.

The excreta didn't fully collide with the air-cooling device until the next day. When we all gathered at our pick-up point,

Bill Williams was waiting for us. Lucky and I arrived together, the last to get there, and as we got closer I could see the veins standing out on Bill's temples. I took this as being not a particularly good sign.

'Yesterday,' said Bill very slowly, forcing each syllable through gritted teeth set in a red face, 'I got a call from the O'Ryan's. They told me they had to call out the fire brigade to an illegal burn-off next to their property. A gorse fire. A *big* gorse fire.' Lucky, Blackass, Carl and I all looked at the ground, trying hard not to giggle.

'They lost a thousand dollars worth of precision fencing. Brand new fencing, that we have to replace.' This was an exaggeration, probably on the O'Ryan's part. True there was a fence there, but it was so old and had it that a hippo could have walked through it without touching the wires.

'Now, you have already been warned,' Bill continued.

Oh shit, here it comes, I thought.

'You are not paid to burn the gorse, you are paid to cut it. I want whoever did it to own up, or else.'

'I did it,' piped up Lucky.

'Right,' said Bill. 'You're down the road. Off you go. And as for the rest of you, any more stunts like that, and it'll be the same for you.' He whirled around and got back into his car, and was gone with a squeal of tyres. I turned around to Lucky, feeling guilty about him taking the rap for me.

'What you do that for?'

'Don't worry about it, bro,' Lucky smiled. He started walking back towards his place, then turned and called back, 'I just get to start my holidays early, eh? See you at the White Hart tonight. Your shout!'

I waved and climbed into the van. Harry was looking at me, not saying anything. I threw a file at him. Darryl revved the van into life, and then we took off for another day on the scheme.

Alana

ALANA WAIRAU'S FATHER ran a disco at the Commercial Hotel on Broadway every Friday night, which meant that she only had to evade his girlfriend to get out. This should have been an easy enough task, as her bedroom was downstairs, next to the games room that had once been the garage. Everything else was upstairs, including the kitchen, the lounge, and the other bedroom - Maggie's territory. Yet somehow Maggie often seemed to know when Alana was sneaking down the driveway, and she would yell out at the top of her wheezy voice, 'and just where do you think you're off to, young lady?'

'Nowhere.'

'Get back inside, then. You know what your father said.'

Alana would skulk back inside, wait until Maggie was busy, then try again. The usual law was three strikes, and she'd get a wallop when her father got home. He didn't mind her friends coming around to the house, where he or Maggie could keep an eye on them, but had expressly forbidden her to go out by herself. Ever since Maggie had found the condom wrapper in the laundry, he had clamped down hard on her. Whenever she protested, he would just tell her that she was only fifteen, and while she lives under his roof, etcetera, etcetera...

But still, roughly every other Friday, Alana managed to sneak away. She would go off in search of Forrest, or Dude, depending on her mood. Forrest lived with her sister, Tania, in a little state house not far away from the hospital where Alana was born. With Forrest there was always boys, while with Dude there was always grass. On a good night, she might strike both.

The second Friday in December, Forrest's boyfriend Mark

had brought around his two cousins, both up for a week from Petone. Tai was fourteen, short and stocky like Mark. Montana was a few inches taller, a few years older, and had a lighter build. As soon as she saw him, Alana could sense the athletic muscle beneath the burgundy shirt he wore. They were all in the sitting room when Alana arrived, listening to Rage Against The Machine. Tania had gone out and left Forrest to babysit.

Dude popped in not long afterwards, but only stayed long enough to share a joint. Forrest and Mark disappeared into Forrest's room, and before long Alana, Tai and Montana could all hear the bed banging against the wall. Tai giggled, and Montana turned the stereo up a bit.

'How'd you get your name?' Alana asked Montana.

'Dad likes cowboy films, Mum likes wine. It was the only name they could agree on.'

'What's your middle name, then?'

'Hugh!' sniggered Tai, ducking to avoid a clip around the ears.

'It's Dad's name,' he explained, his face betraying his dislike of it.

'Mine's May,' Alana said.

'That's alright,' said Montana. He got up to adjust the stereo again, then sat down next to her. She thought that he moved like a cat, and wondered to herself if she could make him purr.

The CD finished, and judging by the silence, so had Forrest and Mark. Tai was prattling on about something, but Alana was not really listening. She was watching Montana. His hand had begun to slowly inch towards her legs. Alana looked up at his face, but Montana's attention was fixed lower down. She had been hoping for something different from him, hoping for at least a smile or a glance, just a touch or perhaps a kiss. Instead, she could already sense an inevitability about what was going to happen. It was there in his silence, and the way his hand hovered ready for action.

She knew that if she was going to stop him, then she had to move now. Staying any longer would be read as a yes. She paused, just for a second, wondering if perhaps this time she had read it wrong, that maybe he was different from the others. Alana was willing him to back off, just a little, and start talking again.

Montana grabbed her thigh and leaned over her. Alana tried to wriggle away, but he just held her tighter and began to climb on top of her.

'No…'

'Why not?'

'I don't want to.'

Montana lifted himself up a little. Alana wanted to think that he *was* different, but there was something in his face that raised doubts. Although his eyes were on her, he didn't seem to be looking at her. It was as if the two were looking into different worlds.

'Tai,' Montana barked. 'Go for a walk.'

Not long after Christmas, well after Montana and Tai had returned to Petone, Alana's period was overdue. She phoned Forrest, who got her to talk to Tania.

'What's the matter with you?' Tania asked, her voice grumpy with concern. 'Didn't you use a rubber?'

'No,' Alana said meekly. She hadn't told anyone what had happened.

'We better get you to the doctor, find out for sure.'

'What'll I tell Dad? Maggie'll kill me!'

'Don't tell them anything. Not until we know. You might just be late, that's all. I'll make an appointment for you at my doctor's and I'll call you. If your Dad asks, just say it's women's stuff. Okay?'

'Okay.'

'You want Forrest to come round?'

'Yeah. I'm scared, Tania.'

'Don't be. We don't really know anything yet.'

When the results came back, they were positive. Alana was due in September. After a few days of panic, she told her father one evening while Maggie was out. His initial fury was dissipated a little by the thought of being a grandfather. She would not tell him who the father was, except that he was from out of town and she didn't think she'd ever see him again. For a moment she thought about telling him everything, but knew he wouldn't believe her. He hugged her and told her not to worry, that he still loved her and would help as much as he could.

He told Maggie later that night, after they had all gone to bed. Alana could hear them fighting upstairs, her father's voice soft and muffled, Maggie's loud and livid.

'I will not have her in this house,' Maggie was yelling. 'She knew the rules and chose to break them. She has to learn to take responsibility for her actions.'

'She's only a kid,' was her father's muffled reply.

'I will not have her in this house. She can go and stay with her slut friends, but the bitch isn't living here. Do you hear me, Roger? She is *not* living here!'

A door slammed, and Alana could hear heavy footsteps marching quickly towards the stairs. She guessed what was coming, and was halfway out the window when she felt Maggie's hands grabbing her by the hair.

'You stupid fucking little whore!' Maggie screamed as she yanked Alana roughly back inside. 'You stupid fucking slut!'

'Leave me alone, you dog-fucking bitch,' Alana screamed back, lashing out blindly, trying to hit Maggie away.

'Don't you fucking swear at me. Don't you fucking swear at me.' Maggie slapped her hard across the face twice. Alana could taste salty blood. She kicked wildly at Maggie, and they both fell over, bouncing off the edge of the bed and on to the floor.

Alana was pinned on the floor, helpless as Maggie hit her in the chest and across the face.

A second pair of hands appeared, clasped Maggie by the shoulders and pulled her off. Alana kicked her in the stomach as she was lifted off, then rolled to the far wall, huddling into a ball from which she stared out at the two figures grappling in the doorway.

'Leave her alone, Maggie,' her father was saying. His voice sounded calm, but he was struggling to hold her back.

'Fuck off. Fuck off and leave me alone!' Alana spat at them.

'You get out of my house, you little slut. Out!'

'Leave her alone, Maggie,' her father said again, dragging her out into the games room and placing himself between them.

Alana stood up defiantly as Maggie glared at her over her father's shoulder. 'I may be a slut, but I haven't sucked as many cocks as you have!'

'That's enough!' her father's voice exploded. He pushed Maggie towards the stairs, then whirled around to Alana. 'Don't you ever talk like that to Maggie again! Understand? Never!'

'She's a fucking bitch!'

Her father stormed across the floor and lifted his hand. Alana cringed, but did not look away. The two scowled at each other. Eventually, the raised hand dropped, limply, to his side.

'You watch your mouth, girl.'

He went back upstairs. He and Maggie fought for a while longer, then there was a silence broken only by Maggie's intermittent sobs. Alana didn't sleep that night.

The next day, her father helped her move in with Tania and Forrest.

On May 20th, Alana celebrated her sixteenth birthday at her father's house. Tania and Dude were there, as were Forrest and her new boyfriend, Theo. Mark had disappeared as soon as he heard what had happened. Maggie and Alana did their best to ignore each other for the whole evening.

On August 28th, Alana gave birth to a girl, Iris Genevieve, who weighed in at just under eight pounds. Her father was working, and Tania could not find Forrest to babysit, and so Alana gave birth alone. Afterwards, still light-headed from the painkillers, the nurse handed her the small, red child. As Alana looked down at Iris, all she could do was wonder *why?*

Floyd

JOY FUSSED ABOUT for ages getting ready for Bryn's 21st. Every ten minutes or so Carol would poke her head through the bathroom door and ask how much longer she was going to be, each time to be answered with a vague shrug of the shoulders. She put on and wiped off four shades of lipstick before she settled on the proper colour. Everything had to look just right. Kere was going to be there.

The woman looking back at her from the mirror looked anxious. Joy practised her relaxed, spontaneous smile, but it took a few attempts to get it looking right. Normally, it would not have been a problem, but this would be the first time she would have seen Kere since they split a few months ago. Actually, she had caught a glimpse of him in the street a few times, but never got close enough to have to sort out whether she was going to say hello or not.

Joy and Carol were originally going to leave at half past seven, but Joy was not ready until almost eight. As Carol almost chased her out to the car, Joy was still vacillating between the black leather jacket and the navy blazer.

'I don't know,' she was saying, 'this goes better with the skirt, but the blazer goes better with my blouse.' She stopped dead beside the car. 'Hang on a minute, Carol. I think maybe I should have worn the black top instead. I'll just go and...'

'Like hell you will. We're late already. You look good, okay? Wear the leather, toss that other one in the back seat, and we're gone.'

'You sure?'

'Trust me. Now, get in the bloody car.'

They climbed in, and Joy tossed the blue blazer over on to the back seat. Carol fumbled about under the seat for the screwdriver.

'If that man of mine doesn't fix this up soon...' she muttered as she forced the screwdriver into the remains of the ignition and gave it a twist. Three attempts later, the engine coughed, then reluctantly agreed to work, prompted by several vigorous revs.

The car was a pink 1973 Ford Falcon, known to all and sundry as Floyd. Carol and John had had Floyd for so long, and it had developed such a unique personality along the way, that the thought of selling or scrapping him had simply never occurred to either of them. Sadly, lately Floyd had deteriorated to such an extent that he was becoming almost impossible to drive. Apart from the stuffed ignition, which was really only an inconvenience, the gearbox was on its way out. First gear had gone completely, and for the last two weeks it had displayed a disturbing tendency to lock itself in reverse. One night, John had been forced to drive backwards for five miles just to get it home. Still, they held on to Floyd affectionately.

Carol tugged Floyd into second gear, got the revs up so he wouldn't stall, and drove off, adding two new scars to the lawn. Joy was fishing about amongst the jumble on the floor, looking for the small bottle of Bacardi she had dropped in there yesterday. When she sat up straight again, she had the bottle in one hand, and was gingerly holding a used condom in the other.

'John's?' she asked. Carol smiled yes. Joy held it up higher to examine it's length. 'I knew he was a big boy, but shit, woman!' She dropped it over the back of the seat, being careful not to let it fall on her blazer. She wiped her hand on the seat, where some foam was showing through the cracked vinyl, then took a hearty swig from the bottle.

'Calm down,' Carol said. 'He's only a guy. You said he didn't mean anything any more. Remember?'

'He doesn't.' A brief pause as she took another mouthful, holding it for a moment, then knocking it back and feeling the comforting warmth spread through her. 'He doesn't. I just...want him to see what he's lost.'

'Uh-huh,' said Carol, sceptically. 'You just remember to keep your knees together around him. Hear me?'

'Hear you.'

By the time they pulled up outside the hall where Bryn's party was being held, Joy was ready. She smoothed out her skirt, adjusting it so it sat evenly, then walked boldly through the door, slightly ahead of Carol. Inside the front door was a short hallway, only ten feet long. The second set of doors were closed, but the noise of the party was pulsing clearly through them. She pushed the right hand door open and slipped into the main room. John was standing only a few feet away.

'About time!' he shouted over the top of the disco, which was playing a Grace Jones number very loudly. 'I thought Floyd might be playing up.'

Carol swept past and planted a kiss on John's cheek. 'Naomi Campbell here had to zip off to Paris for a change of clothes.'

John laughed and draped an arm around Carol, pulling her closer and offering her a bottle of Lion Red. 'You've got some catching up to do,' he said.

Joy looked around the hall. It was full of relatives and acquaintances, the same crowd that seemed to be there wherever she went. She kept telling herself she should move somewhere new, meet different people, but had never gotten around to it. She spied Bryn over by the makeshift bar and eased her way towards him, having to stop every now and then to kiss this aunty or greet that uncle. Bryn was one of her many cousins, and he worked on the mutton chain at the local freezing works. So did Kere.

'Happy birthday, cuz,' she called as she got closer to him.

Bryn looked over and smiled.

'Joy, what a joy!' That was Bryn, same joke for twenty-one years. They hugged and kissed each other on the cheek. 'Is Uncle coming?'

'Nah. Mum phoned to say to wish you a happy birthday and sorry they can't make it. The doctor said he had to rest.'

'Probably just as well, huh? They'd cramp your style a bit, eh? What are you drinking?'

Joy settled for a large gin, and sipped it as she looked around the room again. She couldn't see Kere. Joy mingled for a while, then found herself back by Carol and John an hour and several gins later. Carol leaned over and yelled into Joy's ear, just loud enough so only she could hear.

'John said Kere was here earlier, but took off with Tama and Simon. He reckons they'll be back about ten.'

Joy nodded, trying to look nonchalant. Carol looked at her knowingly, smiled and patted her shoulder. 'Don't worry about him. Have you seen Bryn's mate over there?'

'Which one?'

'That one there,' she said, pointing out a red shirt in the crowd by the bar. 'He's been watching you.' Carol leaned close again. 'He's got a really cute bum!'

Just then the doors swung open, and three men swept into the hall. The second of them was Kere, hair in a ponytail and looking great. Joy stopped in mid-sip, experiencing a strange twinge of *something*. Somebody handed him a bottle, said something, and they all laughed. Joy noticed the way he tipped his head back as he laughed, the way his skin pulled tight across his cheeks. Kere took a gulp of beer and glanced over, waving to John. When he saw Joy, their eyes locked for a few seconds. For that brief moment, the only sound Joy was aware of was the sound of her own body, of her breath and the tempo of her heart. Kere smiled, then turned back to the guys he was with.

At about half past one in the morning, Uncle Terry came over and said she looked like she was ready to go home. The night had not been particularly great, and she had compensated for it by getting well and truly pissed. The red shirt had tried to chat her up, but despite his cute bum had turned out to have all the appeal of day-old chunder. Carol and John had gone home with Floyd about an hour ago, Carol flashing her the secret signal that said *don't come home for a couple of hours*. Kere and Joy had spent the evening skirting around each other without actually talking.

'I can get Aunty to take you home, if you want,' Terry was saying.

'She's right, Uncle,' Joy said. She smiled at him through the ever-increasing haze.

He smiled and shook his head. 'You're just like your Nana, you know that?' he said, and wandered off.

Joy weaved her way to the bar, deciding it was time to move on to the rum. As she picked up her glass, she noticed a familiar ring on the hand next to hers. She looked across at Kere. 'Hello,' she said, as evenly and coolly as she could manage.

'Hi,' he replied. 'How are you keeping?'

'I'm okay.'

'Good.'

There was a pause. Joy toyed with her glass.

'You're looking great,' Kere said.

'Thanks. You too.'

Another pause. More toying with the glass. Kere drank, shuffled about a little. 'So what you been up to?' he asked.

'Not much.'

'Oh. Hey, I noticed that John's gone already. How are you getting home? I mean, I can give you a lift if you want.'

Joy looked up. This was not quite how she wanted it to be, but it was happening. She looked at Kere, trying to read if he had any intentions other than just taking her home.

'Yeah, that'd be cool.'

'Okay. Just give us a call when you're ready.'

'I'm probably ready now.'

They polished off their drinks and left. The cool air outside hit Joy like a wall, and for a while she felt herself tottering on her heels. Kere had a new car, a Jap import that bleeped annoyingly when she opened the door. The drive home, though, was smooth and quiet.

When Joy got up the next morning, Kere was still sound asleep on the sofa. He had decided to spend the night there rather than run the risk of being pulled over by the cops. He had not even hinted about sleeping with her, simply spread himself out on the sofa, said goodnight and fell asleep.

Joy stood at one end of the sofa and looked at him. She had seen him asleep so many times before, but it had never felt as strange as this. There seemed to be something different about him, something in the way his mouth lolled open. She could not think of any words to describe it, just that he did not seem as *together* as he used to. He looked much older than twenty-five. Or maybe, she wondered, it was her that felt older. After all, they had been going together for a very long time.

Somehow, both of them had managed to stumble their way into the sixth form, several years ago now. Kere had first asked her to go out with him as they made their way to English. She said she'd think about it, but was so excited she had trouble concentrating on the play they were studying. It was *Henry V*, and she thought it was unspeakably boring. They had to read the whole thing out in class, and the only thing she could remember about it was how cocky Kere had seemed as he read his part that day, the Constable of France.

He still was cocky, but lately he had started putting on weight and was no longer quite the hunk he had been. Joy took some comfort in knowing she looked better than him now, and yet she felt a strange disquiet. Somewhere in the back of her mind, something was trying to break through, but she couldn't quite get a fix on it. Kere awoke, and squinted at her through sleepy eyes. 'Hi,' she said. 'Sleep okay?'

'Uh, yeah.'

'Good.' Joy turned away and walked to the kitchen to make them both a cup of coffee.

Outside the kitchen window, moistened by dew, Floyd sat sadly on the lawn.

Saving Dave

DAVE WENT TO the Sunday evening church meeting with a friend who used to be on the same work scheme as him, Martin. Dave was quite surprised to see Little John three rows ahead of him, hands waving in the air and speaking in tongues. The last time he had seen him, they had been spotting hash together over a stove in one of the town's more notorious flats.

All the speaking in tongues business didn't really throw Dave, as his mother had been doing it for years. Of course, he had never actually *heard* her, as he had always avoided churches like the plague. But nevertheless, it did not seem out of place. Everyone in the church seemed happy and smiling. Well, almost everyone, but then every crowd has its share of lemons. Everyone hung around for a cup of tea or coffee afterwards, and Dave slipped over to Little John.

'Dave!'

'Dave's not here, man.'

Standard exchange, a favourite piece of Cheech and Chong.

'Man, I didn't expect to see you here,' Dave said, an almost embarrassed laugh evident in his voice. He felt almost as hoha as he did the time one of his schoolmates caught him wanking.

'Same, bro, same,' Little John said. He had a habit of hopping from one foot to the other as he spoke. He waved his hand to indicate the church, and said, 'this place is good for ya.'

'You reckon?'

'Yeah, sure. It's helped me clean my act up, you know? What did you think? Did the tongues freak you out?'

'Nah. Mum's been into it for years.'

'Cool. I tell you what, it sure freaked me first time I came.

But it's cool now, lifting up your hands and praising the Lord.'

Dave nodded uncertainly. The mannerisms were the same, but the man had certainly changed. He just wanted to finish his coffee and get Martin to get him out of there.

'So, are you gonna come again next week?' Little John asked.

Dave knew straight away that a herd of wild horses attached by barbed wire to his testicles wasn't going to get him back next week. It just wasn't his scene.

'Try and stop me,' he said. He had no idea where the words came from, because they were so far from where he was thinking. Now he had said it, though, it was too late to back out.

Martin was busy, talking to the red-headed guy who had been preaching that night. Dave looked around at the people chatting merrily away. There was one other brown face aside from his, a tall guy who looked to be Samoan. Apart from him, it was as white as the Queensland police force. There were two good-looking blondes, who looked to be about sixteen or seventeen, eyeing him coyly from the far side of the room. When he caught their eye, they giggled and looked away. There seemed to be a lot of teenage girls there for the size of the congregation. Martin had actually lured him there by saying that there were two sisters who were absolute physical perfection. Dave couldn't see anyone fitting such high praise, but it was still nicer pickings than the pub had been the night before.

Obviously, he wasn't the only one who thought so. There was another guy, about the same age as Dave, strutting through the gaggle of girls like a rooster with a cork up its butt. He had his hair combed back almost viciously, as if each strand had been terrified into place. He wore a striped shirt and waistcoat that didn't really go together, and flashed a huge, used car salesman smile at everyone who looked his way. He looked like he was trying to look like a film star, but his squint and his almost constant fidgeting with his fly just made him look like a dork.

Finally, Martin took Dave home, but not before Little John

had repeated Dave's remark about coming next week. On the way back to Dave's place, Martin arranged to pick him up next Sunday.

The following Sunday night, Martin and Dave arrived late, and slipped into the back row of the church. The music was pretty bland, but the Samoan dude was playing a nice bass, a genuine Fender Precision. When the red-headed guy got up to preach, he talked about fathers. About having a relationship with the Ultimate Father. Dave compared what he was saying with his own father, a distant man who was always too busy playing sport, too busy watching sport, too busy working, too busy resting, too busy doing the crossword in the Australasian Post.

All through the sermon, Dave could feel something rising up inside him. He tried to stop listening, to think about other things until it was all over. Instead of helping, it just intensified the feeling. Almost before he realised it, everyone was standing, heads bowed, while the red-headed guy asked if anyone wanted to come up the front and give their lives to Christ that night.

'I know there's one here, and you're battling the feelings within you. God would say to relax, to come to Him, and He will carry your burden, He will lighten your load…'

Dave went up to the front. As he walked quickly up the middle aisle, he found himself biting back tears. He could not understand anything that was happening to him. After a few minutes, the red-headed guy came over and got Dave to repeat a simple prayer of repentance, then he laid his hands on Dave's head and began to pray in tongues.

Suddenly, inexplicably, Dave felt like he was beginning to rise up off the floor. Everything around him seemed to be bathed in a warm glow. Not bright or blinding or anything, just *warm*.

'Welcome to the family, son,' the red-headed guy said.

After the service, Martin took Dave to supper at a flash house on the edge of town that belonged to a Dutch couple who were members of the church. It looked like something out of *House & Garden*, everything in just the right place, and nothing tacky or cheap. It was a huge step up from Dave's rat-infested hovel. He decided he could definitely get used to it.

After three months of going to church on Sunday and their youth programme on Saturday, Dave was wondering to himself whether it was all worth it. As soon as he had told her that he had been 'born again', Dave's girlfriend Celestine had dumped him. He had finally met the two Sisters of Perfection, but one was still too young and he had struck out with the other in a major way. Three other girls were all flirting outrageously and competitively, but they were so white and so middle-class that Dave simply did not know what to do around them. They were all pony club princesses.

The Samoan guy had turned out to be Tongan. He got himself into a spot of bother and did a midnight scarper back to Fua'amotu. Dave was now the only non-pakeha in a church of one hundred and twenty. And he felt it.

At first, the differences didn't seem that serious. The youth group came around to his flat for supper one night, and none of them could understand why he asked them several times not to sit on the table or the kitchen bench. One laughed, another thought Dave was calling him fat. The leader of the youth group took him aside and told him that he needed to be set free of the demonic influence of Maori culture. Dave simply did not know what to say back. Maybe he was right.

Little John stopped going to church about that time, and Dave heard through the grapevine that he had scored a large shipment of hash. Martin started going steady with one of the girls, a cute redhead of sixteen. Dave hardly saw him any more. Most of the young guys in the church, Dave thought, were dicks, and the older guys were just scary. About the only person he really got on with was a solo mum named Greer who was about the same age as Dave's oldest sister, and seemed to come from the same kind of background as he had. It was an impression that was confirmed when she told him she had actually marched alongside Dame Whina Cooper in the seventies. She had a daughter of fourteen, who with every month was getting more and more distracting.

The pastor talked to him one night about the need to relate more to the men in the church, and warned him against spending time alone with women.

'Flee temptation,' was his advice.

Dave moved out of his rat-hole and boarded with one of the families in the church. They had three daughters, three of the most obnoxious girls Dave had ever met. On his first day, the father had set out the house rules for him. 'And lastly, and most importantly, you're not allowed in the girls' bedrooms, and they're not allowed in yours. We do have sex, you know.'

Dave knew what he meant even though it was badly phrased. Even so, he could not resist muttering under his breath, 'not with *your* daughters, I don't.'

And so life went on. Dave had no more success in fitting in with the church, yet he remained convinced that that was where he should be. It was good for him, he thought. Just difficult. He learned how to laugh and smile at the right times, when to utter the correct platitudes to keep people off his back. He also kept sneaking out and spending nights on the town with his old friends, having to creep back into the house through an upstairs window early in the morning.

His old friends hadn't changed, but being around them was not the same any more. He felt a little guilty drinking with them, and a lot guilty when he was having his end away. Eventually he realised that he did not fit in with them any longer.

He stuck with the church, largely because he didn't know what else to do. One night he prayed that someone would come along who he could really relate to. Someone who knew where he was coming from. When he opened his eyes, he realised that he was sitting on the kitchen bench.

Lethal Golf

TO CALL THE VON TEMPSKY Memorial Public Links a golf course is probably stretching it a little bit. It would be more accurately described as several rough paddocks with nine squares of mown grass around which low, three-wire fences drooped drunkenly. They were supposed to keep the grazing sheep off the greens, but the hoofprints and droppings on them testified to the fence's inadequacies.

Karl, Gary and Animal played a round there every Friday. They rattled through the gate, the Cortina clanking more than the cattlestop, and shuddered to a stop by the honesty box. While Gary grabbed a scorecard and deposited three two-dollar coins into the box, Karl hauled the golf clubs out of the boot. Animal was fishing about under the seats, stuffing golf balls into the pockets of his black trackpants. He had on a huge white t-shirt, with 'Don't ask me, I don't give a shit!' emblazoned in bright red lettering across his chest.

Gary walked back to the car, and noticed their small collection of clubs leaning against the side of the car.

'Hey, where's the bag?'

'At home,' Karl mumbled. 'Bess had her pups in it on Tuesday and I can't get her out.'

'Hoo, faarck!' said Animal, with a chuckle.

Karl shrugged, gathered the clubs and lofted them onto his shoulder. They only had six clubs between them, a driver, 2 Iron, 5 Iron, 7 Iron, a pitching wedge and a putter, so carrying them would not really be much of a hassle. When they had first started playing, about eighteen months ago, they had been using Gary's wife's clubs. It had been a full Slazenger set she had inherited from her father, but when she left earlier in the year, she had taken them with her. Since then, they had been buying odd clubs here and there as they could afford it.

The three strode over to the first tee. It was a straight, ninety-five metre par three. A competent player could do it in two easily, and both Karl and Gary had managed a birdie here, Gary twice. The only hazard were the cattleyards off to the right, but to get there required a slice so bad that none of them had ever managed it. Animal had come close on a couple of occasions though.

Gary chose the 7 Iron and teed off first. It was a nice clean shot, landing just short of the green, bouncing once before clattering against the middle wire of the fence. According to their rules, that meant he could choose to rehit or take it as it lay. 'I'll take it,' he said.

Animal went next, hooking his shot into the longer grass by the boundary fence. He just shrugged his shoulders, happy with the distance if not the direction.

Karl's shot was much straighter, at least to start off with. Unfortunately, it didn't rise more than a few centimetres off the ground, smacked into something hard in the middle of the fairway - it sounded like a bottle or something - lobbed up a few feet into the air, then stopped dead. It had travelled about twenty metres. Karl muttered something angrily and stomped off.

'Hoo, faarck!' said Animal, with a chuckle.

Karl's second shot was better, but he overshot the green and lost his ball in the bushes behind it. While he searched, Gary completed the hole in par, and Animal in five.

'Call it lost and take a five,' Gary suggested eventually. 'I want to finish today sometime!'

'Smartass,' Karl said, but took the five anyway.

The second hole was a par four, with the road off to the left, and a stunted bluegum in the middle of the fairway. The idea was to either hit over the top of it, or otherwise to go around it. Gary went around, Karl played short. Animal hit it.

By the fourth hole, Gary was up by five strokes. Karl had started to hit them a little cleaner, but did not have the length that Animal had, and found himself one stroke further back. The fifth and longest hole was the site of Animal's triumph. With what all three agreed was probably his best shot ever, Animal succeeded in driving straight on to the green. It was a feat that, as far as they knew, had never been achieved before. All three stood in silence for a while, admiring the majesty of the shot.

'Lethal,' said Karl, with quiet reverence.

Animal eagled the hole in two, gaining three strokes on Gary and leaving Karl six down. They paused for a smoke under the pine trees at the sixth tee. The sixth had a stream that wound around both sides and the back of the green, leaving only a few metres of leeway. There was a self-imposed fine of a dozen bottles of beer for anyone who went into the water from their first shot. As his ball splashed merrily into the stream, Gary groaned and Karl and Animal applauded.

When they lined up for the eighth and penultimate hole, Gary had dropped down two shots behind Animal. Karl was out of the running completely, seven shots behind Gary and having one of his worst rounds ever. Animal teed off first, a grotesque but effective stroke that soared over the herd of sheep grazing in front of them and left him confident of a par. Gary, clean and clinical, landed a few metres behind Animal.

Karl set his ball, then took a few practice swings with the driver. Karl had always been competitive, and being so far behind the other two bugged him intensely. He concentrated deeply, regulating his breathing in an attempt to keep calm and not force his swing too much. He tried to imagine a rod passing through his shoulders, keeping them properly aligned. 'I'm related to…' he began to say.

'...Michael Campbell, yes, we know,' Gary completed his sentence for him. 'He must have got all the golfing skill in the whanau, huh?'

'He's Ngati Ruanui too,' Karl said, ignoring Gary's dig. All the while, he kept practising his swing.

'Are you going to play, or you planning to mow grass all day?' Gary asked.

Karl swung twice more, then stepped closer to the ball and lined up his shot. It was better than his first tee shot of the day, but only marginally. It rose to knee height, and whooshed through the air as fast as a greyhound on heat.

A golf ball is usually a little under 4.3cm in diameter.

A mature ewe's rectum is, roughly speaking, about knee height.

The odds of a golf ball being struck directly into a sheep's anus, even on a course like the Von Tempsky Memorial Public Links, must surely be astronomical. Yet, Karl's *Titleist* ball - one he had fished out of the stream a few weeks prior - disappeared inside a Romney cross at considerable speed. It seemed to home in on the oblivious ewe's backside like a runaway scud missile.

'Hoo, faarck!' said Animal, with a chuckle as the ewe fell to the ground, it's rear end convulsing manically. Karl, Gary and Animal looked at the ewe, then looked at each other. Then they laughed, loudly, until their eyes misted over.

Once they had stopped laughing enough to be able to stagger over to the sheep, it was dead.

'Shit,' said Karl, 'whatta we do now?'

'Call the ball lost,' answered Gary. He looked around to see if there was anyone else on the course. When he was satisfied it was deserted, he swung the carcass over his shoulders and headed towards the Cortina. 'We'll give the round to Animal, okay?' The other two nodded, Karl with somewhat less enthusiasm.

When they got back to the car, Gary dropped the ewe in the

boot, and the clubs were tossed in beside it. They had barely closed the boot when a car pulled in through the gate, driven by an obese old pakeha with a face as red as his Honda Civic.

'Good day for it,' the old man called as he struggled out from behind the steering wheel. 'Have a good round?'

'Lethal!' said Karl as he hopped into the Cortina, accompanied by Animal's chuckle.

The Making of a Town Loony

ELMORE WAS BORN to be the town loony. His father, Manuel, had served the town faithfully for many years, and in the process had left his son a hell of a legacy to live up to. To his eternal credit, Elmore approached his station with a high degree of commitment.

To be a truly great loony, Elmore knew, you need to have a distinctive *modus operandi*. There is a very fine line between a true loony and a madman. There is no credit in being certifiable. A loony, however, fulfils a vital function in the social organism that is a small(ish) town. Part mascot, part entertainer, part admonishment to errant children, a loony cannot be a simple lunatic. A loony must be 'an identity'.

Since June 27th, 1964 - a date that otherwise seems to have no direct significance - Manfred Kakariki had been known as Manuel, had grown a long moustache, and had never been seen without his trademark sombrero, not even by his long-suffering wife, who was ever after to be known as Esmeralda. Her real name was in fact Eunice, but this was a fact that escaped everyone apart from her immediate family.

There was a rumour, which Eunice/Esmeralda refused to confirm, that Manuel even slept with his sombrero on. Her one small victory in life, other than remaining relatively normal in the midst of Manuel's rampant Mexi-philia, was in preventing her husband naming their youngest son Juan Carlos Santa Maria Kakariki. In an elegant bit of subterfuge, she had encouraged Manuel to celebrate the birth of their son with a large bottle of tequila, and when he had passed out, Eunice/Esmeralda had sneaked away and registered him as Elmore John.

Manuel's mania for all things Mexican went beyond the sombrero. From 1969 onwards he drank only genuine Mexican tequila. Anyone he disapproved of became 'damn gringos', and in later years he became much enamoured of carrying a bright orange water pistol with him wherever he went, tucked into two home-made bandoliers he wore across his chest like a bandito.

Representative of his behaviour was an incident when he was asked by a well-meaning woman if he would like to help with a Red Cross door-to-door collection. When offered a small ID badge, he looked at it scornfully.

'Badges? Badges? We don't need no steenking badges. I'll show you what we theenk of badges,' he said, before tossing it away. He then marched up to the first house, pounded on the door and yelled 'Open up, gringos! We've come for your money!...'

A source of sadness for Manuel was that his stomach was unable to handle a Mexican diet, and so he embarked on a campaign to systematically rename all of his favourite foods. So it was that the Kakariki's traditional Tuesday meal of puha, pork flaps and potatoes boiled together in a large pot became Special K Enchiladas.

Young Elmore handled the teasing he got at primary school with exemplary dignity, garnering the praise and support of many of his teachers. He knew, within himself, that his father was not just a nutter, but that he had embarked on a long-standing and noble profession. He quickly began to liken his father's and his own life to that of a priest hearing confession. People could unload whatever was worrying them in the form of abuse or ridicule or laughter, but he remained unaffected, drawing sustenance from his higher calling.

By the time Elmore started high school, he had already begun to display certain traits that his teachers found disturbing enough to warrant calling in the Education Board psychologist. Over the summer holidays of 1982, Elmore had shaved away most of his hair, retaining only a single ponytail sprouting from the back of his head. He had embarked on his own journey. Now, instead of calling his teachers 'sir' or 'ma'am', they became 'most honourable instructor', and seemingly overnight he had developed a speech impediment which caused him to transpose his Rs and Ls. When taken to see the psychologist, he said that he was 'velly solly' for causing any concern.

What was most impressive about Elmore's new persona was that those meeting him for the first time usually took quite a while before they realised that he wasn't really Chinese. It was this that confirmed him as being a true loony, rather than just being a few stones short of a hangi. The first time he quoted Confucius at the dinner table was while they were celebrating Esmeralda's birthday.

'The Master Confucius says, "man who eats kinas is like a bird who farts gold."'

Manuel whooped for joy, spitting out a mouthful of chicken in the process, while Eunice slipped out to the sitting room and downed a quick bourbon to get her through the rest of the meal.

Elmore had an older sister, Gloria, who was taken to live with her aunt a year after Manuel started insisting that the Electoral Office listed him on the roll as *Senõr* M. Kakariki. She had never found it easy dealing with the family's traditions, and the news that Elmore was following proudly in his father's footsteps was the straw that broke the long-suffering camel's back. She started proceedings to have her father committed to a mental hospital, but they found that he was not, by definition, mentally ill.

'He is fully aware of the real world, understands perfectly what he is doing and displays no genuine signs of mental illness,' the psychiatrist had told her and Eunice. 'Granted, his behaviour is very odd, but there is no grounds to hold him in an institution.'

As for Elmore, the Education Board psychologist said almost exactly the same thing. While Elmore had not started to refer to himself by a new, oriental-styled name, his mannerisms and speech were every bit as bizarre as Manuel's. There was, simply put, nothing they could do about either of them.

In 1985, unable to take the shame of it any more, Gloria emigrated to the United Kingdom, where no one would be aware of Manuel and Elmore's growing regional fame. She had been in London for two weeks when she walked into a pub frequented by expatriate New Zealanders and overheard an English guy trying to chat up a Kiwi girl.

'...And there was this Maori guy I met out there who was absolutely convinced he was Chinese. I mean, *absolutely* convinced. Spoke like a Chinaman, looked like one too. Bald except for a ponytail and everything! And get this - someone pointed out his father, and he thought he was a Mexican bandit! Can you believe it?'

Gloria walked straight out again, and the next day boarded the first train for Edinburgh.

Manuel died in September 1993. He had been knocked off his beloved Raleigh Twenty bicycle by a speeding policeman. The incident made headlines throughout the country, especially at first when it was thought that the cop had killed a tourist. After the tangi, Elmore was left to carry on their work alone. Eunice retreated to her family's home at Murupara, reappearing from time to time to make sure Elmore was looking after himself.

By March 1995, Elmore had become disillusioned with being the town loony. So many legitimately insane people were wandering the streets, released by the rapidly closing institutions and left to fend for themselves, that the distinction between him and them was becoming increasingly blurred in many people's minds. At the end of February he noticed that the kids who once used to follow him everywhere now avoided him fearfully.

By April, he had decided it was time to call it a day. He packed up his belongings, bid farewell to his few remaining friends, shaved off his ponytail and moved to Christchurch, where he found a job as a security man at the new casino. They hired him because he seemed very knowledgeable about Asia.

Aunty Huriata and the Seven Angels

OVER AT THE CORNER table, Aunty Huriata was regaling the faithful with tales of angels. Faces filled with hope nodded in wonder, their eyes shining with eagerness. Cups of tepid tea sat forgotten before them, leaving their doleful rings on the green painted chipboard tables.

In the kitchen, a couple of the boys were helping themselves to a late kai, swallowing mouthfuls of microwaved stew between talk of work and women and whether the league season would ever get started. From time to time, they would poke their heads through the serving hatch and snigger at Aunty Huriata. She was now on to the time she saw the seven angels early one morning at Ratana.

Cherry sailed across the floor of the wharekai as only she could, leaving in her wake an essence that was two parts Chanel, one part tobacco. 'If you ever see those angels again, Aunty,' she said as she passed the table, 'make sure you check out their 'equipment' for me.'

The boys in the kitchen giggled and turned away. Aunty and the faithful carried on as if Cherry had never existed. Aunty was up to the part where her younger cousin Esther had woken her up, nudging her in the ribs with her small, sharp elbows and asking her to turn off the lights.

Cherry joined the boys in the kitchen, comparing favourite nightclubs as she rummaged through the cupboards for an ashtray. She gave up, humphing in exasperation as she went to stand just outside the open doorway, flicking ash on to the gravel driveway. She had tried a few times to quit smoking, but the nervousness she felt about her operation had enticed her back with renewed fervour. The operation loomed before her like the crumbling cliffs of Ohawe, disintegrating in the fierce Taranaki southerlies. The surgeon's scalpel would soon bare her to the world, draw her from the womb afresh, so that with her new birth even Aunty could no longer call her Charles. Yet with this new birth came a new vulnerability, and also a degree of loss.

Little Esther and young Huriata, transformed to youth by Aunty's oratory, were sitting up in their bed now. The shining faithful were smooth-skinned with hope, letting Huriata's voice wash over them, baptising them in the glow of a sixty-year-old revelation. With the miraculous eyes of true believers, they too could see the seven angels, standing in wedge formation at the foot of the bed. They too held their breath in awe, as the glowing figure in the centre beckoned towards Esther with one golden hand...

From the doorway, looking out from the kitchen across the driveway to the hills, Cherry could only hear the occasional word. It mattered little. She had heard the story many times, over and over for the last thirty years. She knew it by heart, could see it in her head as clearly as she could see father's face, downcast and whakama. She had longed for angels to appear then, to fill the musty sitting room with their presence. All there had been was her father's long silence and the rustle of his newspaper. Cherry had chosen the wrong time, she knew. Angels can't be seen in the harsh light of noon. They materialise in the morning mists, weaving the half light of dawn to the departing stars so that the day may be pulled gently from the earth. Then they would return with the dusk, watching over the houses, guarding the specks of enclosed light from the deeper darkness.

'Haere mai, e wairua, haere mai.' At the corner table, Aunty Huriata dropped her head and gazed at her hands, gnarled and stringy, so unlike the angel's. The faithful let their heads fall as well, and a quietness settled upon the wharekai. Only the boys in the kitchen moved, spreading butter on their bread and talking. They seemed oblivious to the thickening of the air.

Aunty Huriata spoke, her voice soft and slow. She resumed her tale, recounting the way the middle angel had taken Esther's hand for a moment. The smile, Aunty said, seemed to warm the room and scatter the shadows. Then the seven angels lifted like a mist, dispersing at the foot of the bed into wisps that floated away through the walls and the ceiling. Aunty had sat and watched, then turned to Esther, who was already asleep. Soon she too had drifted off into peaceful, pleasant dreams.

Cherry took one last drag on her cigarette, contemplated its glowing tip for a moment, then tossed it on to the driveway. Its smoke left a shallow grey arc that drifted away, leaving the butt's final resting place unmarked. She wondered whether to go for a walk, or to return to the wharepuni, past Aunty Huriata and her apostles. Before she even realised she had decided, Cherry was already crunching along the gravel. As she passed by, the angel at the top of the tohu seemed to hide its face from her. She was unsure if it was an omen, or an act of shame.

Esther had been dead in the morning, of course. When Aunty had awoken, Esther's body was already cold. It always seemed to work that way. In the act of giving, they always seemed to take.

The Farewell Place

IT WAS THE LAST day of the tangi, and they had taken the old man's casket out on to the porch of the wharenui. It was a hot day, especially for September in Taranaki, and Kahu could see small beads of sweat forming on the brows of the black-clad kuia. From where he stood, behind and just to one side of the casket, he could glance out over the people, gathered loosely together like a flock of black and grey birds, further out past the fields embroidered with boxthorn and windswept macrocarpa and on towards the hills rolling gently up into the low blue sky. The wharenui faced away from the sea, and the porch where he stood was in the lee of the soft breeze that ruffled the purple scarf of the Ratana priest. For the fifth time in as many minutes, Kahu wished he could understand what the priest was saying, just so he could get some idea of how much longer he had to stand there in the hot, thick air.

The whanau had decided earlier that the elder grandsons, Kahu included, would be the pallbearers, and Kahu's mother had eventually persuaded him to put on a tie as a show of respect. He forced a finger between his neck and the too-tight collar, hoping that even a little cool air would start to circulate inside the sweaty confines of the shirt. Earlier, while he was dressing in the damp concrete toilet block, he had inadvertently splashed quarter of a bottle of aftershave on it, and had to wear a blazer to cover the stain. Now the fumes were rising and entwining his throat like a python, squeezing the oxygen from him and making his head swim. Kahu fought against the black tide with all his might, willing himself not to faint as he had at Aunty Kuini's tangi the year before.

The priest had started the final prayer now, and Kahu followed the cue as everyone around him bowed their heads. He mumbled 'Amene' in unison with the congregation, and lifted his head. He could hear Ripeka sobbing over to his left. For the first time he noticed how the glare of the sun had created a haze over the gate and the shamble of cars parked along the narrow roadway. Ripeka's crying seemed closer now, but Kahu himself felt nothing except the desire to be out of the sun and the crowd and to be someplace where he could breathe freely. He wore the sad and solemn face of the mourner. He wished he could cry, that he could feel genuine grief for the loss of his grandfather, but nothing would come. He felt guilty not only for that, but also for how his mind had wandered during the priest's long and indecipherable sermon. He had nodded and smiled and shaken his head sadly at the right moments, but had been thinking of last night's sneaking off to the pub in town, and later fumbling in the park with Cathy, his cousin Gina's friend from school.

Someone tapped him on the shoulder. Uncle Gene, with Ripeka half buried in his shoulder, stood behind him. 'It's time, boy. Go by Koro so they can take him to the hearse.'

Kahu fumbled his way towards the waiting undertaker. He felt the hand of one of the kuia briefly grasp his elbow as he passed, and he felt something indescribable conveyed in the gentle touch. He paused long enough to turn and offer a smile. It had been old Wanihi; for the last four days she had been chuckling and swapping stories with whoever would listen, but today the sparkling eyes were raw. She nodded twice and then waved Kahu on. The undertaker was a small and sombre-looking pakeha, with wrinkled skin that seemed to be laced with silver. He guided Kahu to the head of the coffin, alongside Kevin. To the accompaniment of a wail that chilled Kahu despite the heat, he and five of his cousins carried Morehu Campbell Te Kaho to the waiting Buick.

For the last five days, up until the time it had been taken outside, the casket had been lying open at the back wall of the wharenui, and Morehu had been continually fussed over by his two eldest daughters, Huriata and Kay. Kahu had slept along the wall to Morehu's right, sandwiched uncomfortably between the towering bulks of his father and Uncle Gene. It was close enough that several times during the four nights his feet had rapped against the casket.

In life Morehu had been dark and hyperactive. Age had not slowed him - rather it had given him the freedom from responsibilities that he had sought all his life. There had been about him a hedonistic air that Kahu had found irresistible. Together they had snuck away from their disapproving family to smoke and drink together when Kahu was fifteen. Only two years ago.

Everyone had said how peaceful the old man looked, how at rest he must be. To Kahu, he looked colourless and empty like a discarded plastic bag. The skin that had once been as brown as polished wood was now a drab shade somewhere between grey and rust. This was not the Koro he had known. Somewhere, lost amongst the death and the embalming fluid, Morehu had been drained away along with the blood in his aged veins. Kahu had seen the life start to seep away after Morehu's third stroke, but the first sight of his corpse still shocked him.

By the end of the second night, Kahu had decided that when people looked into the tangible face of death, they saw that which they believed the dead most desire, whether it be youth or peace or some kind of resurrected life.

'He still looks so *alive*!' Ripeka had whispered on the third day.

A fourth bus load of mourners had just passed through, and Kahu and Ripeka had dutifully greeted them all. There had been one girl who he had thought was a genuine babe, but he didn't fancy tracking her down just to discover she was yet another cousin he hadn't met before. He decided it was safer to persevere with Cathy. Kahu closed his eyes and remembered Koro stumbling home, balanced precariously on his walking stick and stinking of gin and urine.

On the third night everyone had gathered to share their memories. Most had spoken in Maori, and Kahu, Ripeka and Gina had huddled together in the far corner.

'I know why Maoris have flat noses,' Ripeka whispered. 'Too much hongi-ing!'

They had all giggled and Gina had elbowed Ripeka in the ribs. On the adjacent mattress, Kevin was glowering sternly at them. He was always serious, and the threesome ignored him.

'When you hongi, always check for pimples on their nose,' Kahu had said, and then made a graphic squelching noise.

'Oh, gross.' Gina wrinkled her nose.

'And never kiss a woman with a beard,' he added.

'Or an old man with sideburns,' Ripeka said. It was her turn to wrinkle her nose.

Kevin shushed them grumpily, and they were quiet for five minutes or so. Then, just as the Ratana priest had stood to speak, Gina leaned over.

'I gotta go.'

'What?'

'I gotta go take a leak.'

'Well, go then,' Ripeka said.

'I can't,' Gina said, gesturing to the only door that stood at the far end of the wharenui. 'Everyone will see me. Come with me.' She tugged at Ripeka's sleeve.

'Go yourself. They're all listening to the minister. If you crawl down the middle quietly they'll never notice.'

Gina persuaded Ripeka to go with her. They had barely gone six feet before Gina knocked someone's suitcase over with a thump. Kahu clamped his hand over his mouth to stifle a chuckle as the two girls crawled their way along, knocking bags and feet and rolled up blankets aside. By the time they reached the door they were both giggling uncontrollably, and as they got outside there were loud shrieks of relieved laughter.

Today was the last day, and behind him, Ripeka was crying inconsolably. The contrast struck Kahu like a heavy blow to the chest. He started to feel sadness, but it was more for Ripeka's grief than any sorrow of his own. The funeral procession had made its way to the cemetery, and the coffin had been carried to the grave. The old man was surprisingly heavy, and for the last fifteen metres Kahu had struggled with the load, dreading the thought of dropping him. He had made it, but his arm tingled and felt terribly weak.

They were burying Morehu on top of Nana, and alongside Aunty Kuini. Kahu could remember being four years old, gazing at the shiny, flower-strewn box deep down in this same hole and wondering what it all had to do with Nana Te Kaho. It seemed a very long time ago. He had never cried for her.

Once the casket was lowered, Aunty Huriata carefully placed a suitcase and a bottle of Gordon's Gin in the grave. Kahu recalled his first taste of gin, stolen from Koro's glass one Christmas. For some reason he couldn't understand, he also remembered kissing Cathy last night, as they tucked themselves into the shadows of the tunnels at the park.

Kahu's father nudged him and nodded towards the grave. A line had formed and was slowly passing the foot of the grave. He could hear the soft clatter of soil hitting the casket. Kay and Ripeka were up ahead and were somehow managing to hold each other upright as their bodies quaked with grief. For a moment Kahu felt a kind of jealousy, but soon it was overtaken by the same guilt he had felt earlier. The line shuffled its way to the farewell place.

When it was his turn, Kahu looked down at the coffin. The dirt in his hand felt cool and dry, and he rubbed it slowly in his palm. Beneath the dirt and the polished wood, beyond the satin lining and the brass handles, lay the bodily remains of Morehu Campbell Te Kaho. But there felt as if there was a huge gulf between the grandfather and the grandson, more than just years or space or air or earth. The old man was dead.

It was then that Kahu felt the gift that Wanihi had given him, that indefinable something in her grasp when she had taken his elbow. He felt it growing inside him, like a shoot tunnelling its way up through the soil towards the light of a hot spring day. He knew now that although there would be no new memories for him, Kahu could keep as much of his Koro as he needed.

Swimming

CINDY WAS ALMOST seventeen that summer, and was already tired of people telling her she looked like Kiri Te Kanawa. Sure, her hair was a little frizzier, and her lips a little fuller, but otherwise the resemblance was uncanny. The only thing was, Cindy absolutely loathed opera. 'Whitey moaning,' she'd call it, and we'd giggle and make ghastly, agonised yelpings.

I had just turned eighteen, and was impossibly thin. Oh, the days when youthful energy managed to hold off generations of fat genes. There are still times when I long for the summer when I was young, good-looking and trim, instead of chubby, windswept and interesting. There are still times when I long for Cindy.

About half past ten one particularly warm night, we decided to go skinny dipping in the high school swimming pool. We grabbed a couple of towels, my tape deck and a few tapes (*Kaya* and Randy Crawford if I remember correctly), and walked around to the school. It was a very clear night, and a crescent moon smiled its Cheshire cat smile at us as we ambled along. I cradled the deck in front of me with one arm, and draped the other across Cindy's shoulder. She held me close to her by my waist, and her hand reached around to gently stroke the front of my hip as we talked.

We talked about all sorts of things, but nothing seemed important. It was warm, and for the moment we had everything we wanted or needed. When *Secret Combination* played, Cindy sang along, soft and slightly off-key. I remember looking across at her, and feeling my heart swell at the sight of her smile. We took the short cut, pausing as we crossed the bridge over the town's pathetic excuse for a stream. We stopped long enough to change tapes and for Cindy to light a cigarette. Then it was up the small hill and across the road into the school.

When we got close to the pool, we turned the music off. One of the teachers lived in a house that backed right on to the pool, and we didn't want to wake him up. Cindy said he was a nice guy, a pastor in one of the churches in town, but he probably wouldn't take kindly to a couple of teenagers swimming naked in the school pool in the middle of the night.

Clambering over the gate was, for me, always the worst bit. It was not very high, only a few inches taller than me, but it was made out of smooth steel uprights with only the one crossbar, which was at eye level. What was worse was that it was topped off with seven sharp spikes that seemed to shudder with delight at the thought of puncturing my bum.

Cindy slithered over easily, and waited on the far side with a wry grin as I tenderly made my way. 'Don't worry,' she said. 'If you hurt anything, I'll kiss it better.'

'Promises, promises.'

It wasn't until a few years later that it struck me as amusing the strange little conventions we maintain, even in quite intimate circumstances. That night, in the shadows of the gymnasium that opened on to the pool, Cindy and I shed our clothes and slipped quietly into the cool water from opposite sides. We made an elaborate show of not taking any great interest in each other, but still caught each other stealing glances.

Once we were in, we lowered ourselves until the water lapped about our chins. Cindy smiled, pointed to the far end of the pool, and then slipped beneath the water like a blade. I stayed where I was, watching her shadow slice its way to the far end of the pool and back again. She completed almost two lengths underwater, surfacing close by. The water held back her hair and glimmered on her smooth shoulders, giving her the look of some magical mermaid.

'Why didn't you come with me?' she asked.

'I'm still getting used to the water. She's a bit cold.'

'Wimp.'

Her lips spread in a smile, and I could see the starlight glinting off her teeth. Straight, perfect, model teeth. I self-consciously pressed my own lips together as I smiled back, hiding the crooked jumble of fillings that had the odd tooth wrapped around it.

'It's okay for you. You don't have external genitalia.'

She laughed, and reached out with one hand to run her fingers across my cheek. Then she leaned away and floated off slowly on her back. Only her face and the tips of her breasts showed above the water, painted by the ethereal light of the overhead stars. The moon had half-hidden itself behind one of the classroom blocks, peeking at us coyly. I floated after her.

Once we had swum a few slow lengths together, we leaned against the wall of the pool closest to the gymnasium. I stood, so that the water came up to just above my navel. Cindy had her feet on the bottom of the pool a few feet in front of her, so that her only her head and shoulders were clear. The sensation of the cool water and the warm air against naked skin was delicious.

'Do you think we should have called Tiff to see if she wanted to come?'

'Nah,' Cindy said. 'She makes too much noise.'

I knew she was right. Once Tiff started laughing, it seemed nothing short of unconsciousness could stop her. Still, I felt a little guilty about not including her. The three of us normally did everything together.

'Do you think she's got a nice bum?' Cindy asked.

'Huh?'

'You heard. You're a male. You've looked.'

'Ouch. Caught!' We chuckled. 'Yeah, it's not bad, but on her it looks a little strange.'

'How do you mean?'

'Well, on most girls it would probably look great, you know, nice shape and stuff, but the rest of Tiff is so skinny that it just looks too big for her. It's kind of like, I dunno, like putting a horse's ass on a goat.' Cindy laughed. 'Don't you dare tell her I said that. I mean it's cute, but it's just the wrong size for the rest of her.'

Cindy turned around, put her hands on the side of the pool and lifted herself up until the water covered her only from her knees down. 'Is mine better?' she asked.

I just stood there and looked at her for several seconds. She was the nearest thing to perfection I had ever seen. 'Yes,' I finally said. 'You have a gorgeous bum. Just like the rest of you.'

She lowered herself back down but stayed standing, turning towards me. She held out her arms, and I came towards her. Cindy smiled as she slid her arms under mine and reached up and placed her hands on the back of my shoulders.

'You are a very sweet boy,' she said, and gently pulled us down into the water. Her legs slipped up and encircled my waist, and as she held me tightly she kissed me gently on the chin.

'I could stay here all night.'

'Maybe so, but be careful,' Cindy said, wriggling her hips so that she bumped against my growing erection. 'You might sink us both with that thing if you're not careful.' She kissed me once more, and then we just embraced silently.

I did not try to make love to her. It would have been unnecessary. Cool water, warm air, soft flesh. The feel of her breasts against my chest as they swelled with each deep breath. The smoothness of her thighs around my hips, the roughness of her heels against the small of my back. The sharpness of her jawbone beneath her skin, nestled in the crook of my neck. So many sensations, so much to take in and store away for future memories.

'I love you,' she said; finally, before disentangling herself and swimming across to the ladder. I waited until she was out and beginning to towel herself down before I got out. I walked past her quickly to my pile of clothes, feeling strangely embarrassed about my hard-on. We dried and dressed in silence, clambered back over the gate and wandered across to the playing fields.

We lay down in the middle of a soccer field, just inside the centre circle. Cindy lit a cigarette and I turned the Bob Marley tape on again. We lay close together, looking up at the thousands of stars in the sky. *'You make me feel like a sweepstakes winner...'* Bob sang in the still air.

Sometimes when you look at a clear night sky, the stars seem to be holes in a dark cloth, or spots floating in black, inky liquid. That night, they looked more like what they really were - balls of light floating in nothingness. Thousands of individual moments that together made a wonderful whole.

In the periphery of my vision, I could see the red glow of Cindy's cigarette. I rolled over on to my side and placed my hand on her belly. I leaned my head close to hers so that I could feel the warmth that radiated from her skin, kissed her softly where her neck met her jaw, just below her ear.

'Arohanui,' I whispered, then rolled over on to my back again.

'Arohanui,' Cindy whispered back, and her hand gently clasped mine.

And there we lay, that summer night too many years ago, gazing up at the thousand burning stars.

Tiri

THE DESIRE TO HURT someone, anyone, is incredibly strong. It sits within me like a cold iron weight. From outside, the darkness just throbs, pressing against my flesh until I can physically feel it. Black and bitter.

It was always like this. Battling against the slow-burning fury, trying to contain it. Ever since I was a small child, not allowed to play with the other kids in the street because my skin was not the same colour as theirs, because my old man worked in a freezing works instead of a shop or an office, because my clothes were made out of the remains of my sisters' dresses and the other kids would laugh at me and call me the black beggar. And I would fight them, and even though I was smaller and frailer than them, the fury and the pain on the inside would place steel in my fists and my muscles and I would force them to the ground and pound away at them until they cried and blood started to trickle from their nose or their mouth. Being kids, we always stopped at the sight of blood. Victory had been proved.

When Dad got home and was told that I had been fighting again, he would take me out to the back porch and belt me with the jug cord. When I was twelve, and had started to grow, I had a go at him with a piece of timber that had been left on the back doorstep. Once he got over the initial shock, he prised the wood off me and beat me until I just lay still, curled up into a tight, sobbing ball half way under the tattered porch. As he walked away, I whispered '*black bastard, fucking black bastard*', over and over again.

Two years later, when Dad was drunk and sitting flopped

over the kitchen table, I laid into him for all that I was worth. It was the first time ever that I was able to escape from that darkness that always hovered over me. As I felt his nose shatter beneath my fist, blood and fragments of teeth splatter and grind between my clenched fingers, I had never before been so high and so happy. It was like everything inside me just emptied out on the old bastard.

Afterwards I ran off. Never went home again. I stayed on the street for three months before Social Welfare caught me and put me in a foster home. I took off from there when I was sixteen. A takapui merchant seaman smuggled me into Sydney in return for a blow job each night of the trip. It wasn't worth it, because I got arrested on my first night there and deported straight back. Put it down to experience, they said. And don't come back.

And always the darkness just wrapped itself around me, black and bitter.

I can't remember the first one's name. She was white, some Daddy's girl from a posh school who wanted to piss off her olds for not giving her another horse or something. She started to hang around the spacies joint, eyeing up the guys and trying to look like she'd been smoking for years. I took her out into the alley out the back and did her. Once I was in, the silly bitch started to cry and ask me to stop. I punched her in the soft part of her belly a few times and told her to shut the fuck up. She closed her eyes and her mouth, but the sight of the tears falling down her cheeks just pissed me off. She was weak and stupid. 'What the fuck did you expect?!' I yelled at her. 'Fucking violins?!'

I made her do what *I* wanted, and it felt good. I thought about my old man, and about the teachers at school, and all the other assholes who made me do what they wanted 'cause I was just some dumb blackass, and then I looked down at this rich white bitch doing what *I* told her, and I wrapped the darkness around her as well. When I was finished, I warned her that if she told anyone, I would kill her.

When I got Mere pregnant we had to get married because she was from some respectable Tuhoe family, and if I didn't her uncles were gonna cut my ure off. She had a boy, which she named after her father. We stayed together for about two years, and then she walked out when she caught me in bed with her cousin. I wasn't all that worried, 'cause we never really liked each other. It had all just started as a poke in the dark.

Always in the dark. By then, daylight seemed almost foreign, only any good for getting pissed. The night was where I lived. In the shadows, I could convince myself that the darkness was gone, and that I really was free.

It was Vanessa that changed it all. She didn't care about the old things, or worry about what would happen next. She taught me how to enjoy now, to force aside the darkness and live. I actually loved her. I even stopped screwing around, stayed faithful. Tried hard to make her happy too. Got a proper job, collecting rubbish for the council. She was into reading and shit, got me into writing things down when I was feeling hoha. It seemed to work, too. The darkness started to weaken, like the half hour before dawn. It was great. For the first time ever I could imagine growing old. And I liked it.

Then, just recently, things started getting a bit tight. The car broke down and we had no money to fix it. Stuff like that. So Vanessa decided that she better get a better paying job, and so she moved down to Te Kuiti to work in her brother's shearing gang as a rousie. Just a few months, she said, and then we'd go to Brisbane, see what it was like over there.

Yesterday, all the council workers went on strike so I borrowed a mate's bike and went down to Te Kuiti to surprise her. It had been raining heavily for the last few days, so I guessed that they probably weren't shearing.

They weren't. She wasn't at her brother's place, but his wife said they all went to a party the night before, and she might have crashed there for the night. She gave me an address, and I cruised around. Vanessa was there, in bed with some fella.

The darkness crashed in like the world was ending. Honestly, I can't really remember much except the feeling. Like you've just had your balls chopped off and everyone in the world is standing there laughing at you. Dumb blackass.

I'm not sure, but I think they're both dead. It probably won't take long for the pigs to put two and two together. Every time I close my eyes, all I can see is Vanessa's normally beautiful naked body crumpled up on the floor, tangled and ugly in the pale blue sheets, blood everywhere.

And all around me is the darkness. Nothing's changed since I was a kid. Nothing ever will change. Just the same old shit, over and over again, just with different names or faces. I can't live with it any more. There's just no point. There's no escaping it, black and bitter.

I leave this behind for my son. I know it aint much, but it's more than my old man left me. I hope you learn something from it when you're old enough. Please don't think of me as a coward or just some dumb blackass.

Stay away from the darkness.